D1741532

QL

THE EXPEDITION

When the widow Doña Elena Alvarado y O'Bryan lost horses to renegade *bandoleros* out of Mexico, she hesitated about sending her riders in pursuit. As it turned out the same border-jumpers had raided other ranches belonging to *norteamericanos*. They organized to go to Mexico in violation of the law, and bring back their horses. And also teach the renegades a lesson. However, down in Mexico things didn't turn out as expected. It was a daunting experience for the Americans, hazardous in the extreme; that any got back alive was a marvel, that all of them got back, and brought with them a wounded Mexican woman, was little short of a miracle.

THE EXPEDITION

John Hunt

CHIVERS LARGE PRINT
BATH

British Library Cataloguing in Publication Data available

This Large Print edition published by Chivers Press, Bath, 1994.

Published by arrangement with Robert Hale Limited.

U.K. Hardcover ISBN 0 7451 2004 0
U.K. Softcover   ISBN 0 7451 2016 4

Photoset, printed and bound in Great Britain by
Redwood Books, Trowbridge, Wiltshire

THE EXPEDITION

CHAPTER ONE

HORSETHIEVES

'*Bandoleros*,' the old man said, straightening up from his study of horsetracks in the pale desert soil. He was the colour of mahogany with startlingly white hair. His dark eyes had muddy whites. He was wiry-lean, thin-lipped and left an impression of agelessness. His name was Batista Moraga del Hidalgo. 'Hidalgo' came from the village ten miles southeast where five generations of Moragas had been born and died.

He finished his study of the empty land, turned with a slight shrug and raised his eyes to the woman sitting the blood-bay horse with four white stockings. She had grey at the temples, otherwise her hair was ebon black to match the unsmiling eyes set in a flawless face of rare symmetry.

The old man said, '*Señora*...?'

She finally looked down at him. 'Yes, I heard you.' Unlike the old man her English had no trace of an accent. 'But not towards the border this time.'

Batista Moraga agreed. 'No, this time they don't expect to be chased. They are *malos hombres*. And bold. This time they will make a bigger raid, up around the ranches over by

1

Hidalgo then down to the border and across it.'

'How many, Batista?'

Moraga looked down again. 'Maybe fifteen this time. I said, they are getting bolder.'

The handsome woman nodded. 'And stronger. Next time maybe thirty.'

Moraga turned to snug back his cinch. 'Or fifty. *Señora*, I have seen it happen many times during my life. When there is a revolution down in Mexico, the refuse from both sides raid up here.'

She raised her left hand, waited until he was mounted then turned back. 'How many horses; did you get a count?'

Moraga hadn't. No one could in open range country. Not for weeks, maybe months. But he made a guess based on where their saddle stock had been and how many had been in one herd.

'Thirty. Maybe fifty. Enough to cripple us, *Señora*.'

She rode with the sun behind her, to her right a little so that it caught her profile. She was a stunning woman, not young and without a wedding band. She was the widow of Henry Alvarado whose grandfather, a soldier of Spain, had been granted all the land between the settlement of Hidalgo, west to the crumpled, dim-hazed mountains. North only about three hundred miles. No

2

one had ever marked the boundaries. There had been no need. The ranch of the Alvarados had title to nine year-round springs and a creek that came out of the ground a hundred miles north and coursed crookedly the full length of the ranch. As far as anyone knew there was no other surface water in the area. The long-dead soldier of Spain who, as part of some forgotten expedition of exploration, had been shrewd enough to realise that whoever owned the water controlled the land, had accepted his grant and had moved on to it, but about all he had contributed in the way of improvements was the massively walled, low and rambling fortress-like residence. He had tried raising horses. Indians had killed his *vaqueros*, stolen most of his animals, and what they did not get marauders up out of Mexico got.

The dead husband of the present *señora*, Elena Alvarado y O'Bryan, had hired riders who used weapons as well, sometimes better, than ropes, hobbles and branding-irons. As a result he had fulfilled the dream of the soldier of Spain; the ranch of the Alvarados raised and sold the finest horseflesh between Texas and California.

This was the first large-scale raid since the death of the *patrón* four years earlier. As the lady and her *mayordomo* rode in silence back to the big yard with its large old cottonwood trees, its dust and corrals and outbuildings which included a very large, low adobe barn and scattered *jacals* for the married *vaqueros*, Batista stole an occasional sidelong look at her. Shortly before they entered the yard he said, 'I think this time they will steal many horses. Their course is in the direction of the *gringo* ranches. Maybe they will get a hundred, maybe two hundred.'

She turned as she listened. Since coming to the ranch as a bride she had learned a lot, not just about horse-ranching but about the natives. Batista was expounding one of his ideas. Her husband, who had laughed at her Irish impatience, had told her to listen. To wait, to be patient, because his people considered *yanqui* bluntness the epitome of bad manners. So she looked at the old man and waited. This time it was no effort, but there were times when she had to lock her jaws to keep from telling someone to get to the point. It did no good, they stubbornly explained in their own way, in their own time, according to their custom.

Batista's narrowed eyes were shrewd as he faced her with a bitter smile. 'If they run off very many *gringo* horses, it will be their mistake. The *gringos* do not take such losses philosophically—as part of the price for living near the border.' The shrewd old eyes neither blinked nor wavered. 'They will go after those *bandoleros*. As many of them as

4

there were raiders. Maybe even many more.'

Elena entered the yard thinking of this. As she was turning away after a *remudero* had come to lead her horse to the barn, she said, 'I hope so, Batista,' and walked in the direction of the massive fortress of a house with its walled patio and grilled windows.

Batista sat on the old bench along the barn's front wall and removed his spurs with their oversized Chihuahua rowels. He looked up as a shadow fell close by. The barrel-built man with a heavily pock-marked face said, 'Well?'

Batista shrugged. *'Bandoleros.* A large party of them. They didn't go south, they rode northward on a large sweep.'

The pock-marked man blew out a big breath. 'Towards Hidalgo?'

'Yes. In that general direction.'

The pock-marked man grunted down on to the bench and settled himself comfortably by shoving out both legs in the dust. 'Do we go after them, Batista?'

'She didn't say.'

The other man, younger, powerfully built from the waist up, looked bleakly across the yard in the direction of the house. 'When will she say? They will be two-thirds of the way to the border. It's not like stealing cattle, which cannot be run hard.'

Batista leaned back dangling his spurs from a dark hand. The man at his side,

Epifanio Garcia, called 'Pifas', had been one of the dead *patrón's* *pistoleros*. He feared nothing that rode, walked or ran, and although he was probably in his forties now, he was still a man of violent thoughts. Batista said, 'By tomorrow, if I know her, she will be angry enough.'

Epifanio Garcia cleared his throat and spat, then pushed up to his feet to walk away. Batista stopped him. 'Pifas; don't grumble to the other men.'

Garcia's sweat-shiny face darkened, but he said nothing. He simply stood gazing at the *mayordomo* for a bitter moment then walked away.

Batista watched his bow-legged, rolling walk and gently wagged his head.

The *remudero* who had cared for their horses came to lean in the barn doorway. He was young, almost fair, with an unlined face and a supple, lithe build. He was one of the best horsebreakers in the country. His name was Ramon Cruz. He too watched Pifas Garcia for a moment then quietly spoke. 'Do you know what he is thinking?'

Batista knew. 'Yes. But the *patrón* is dead. He is not here to round up riders and go after the horses.'

Ramon Cruz smiled softly at the old man. '*Viejo*,' he said patronisingly. 'With your patience you should have been a priest.'

It was the wrong comment. Batista looked

6

up, then got to his feet to face the younger man. His nostrils flared and his dark eyes smouldered. 'When I was your age I learned not to open my mouth to patronise people. Do you know how I learned that?' He swung the spurs too swiftly for the younger man to move clear. They missed his face but tore his shirt to the navel. 'That's how they taught me and I still have the scars. You're lucky, you had a shirt.'

Batista stamped away leaving Ramon Cruz to consider his ruined shirt. The rowel marks were no more than pink scratches.

The day was ending. Aromatic mesquite smoke rose from several chimneys around the yard, including those at the *patrón*'s residence.

A sun made saffron by dust in the dry air was gathering its farthest remnants very slowly, pulling them westward as the sun went lower with immeasurable slowness. A desert autumn had shorter days than those of full summer. Even so daylight lingered a long time, usually until well past suppertime. Usually before late dusk someone came out of a *jacal* to sit on a bench with a guitar. Except for gala times which included holy days, times for local celebrations when the music was fiery to feed passionate souls, the songs were about misfortunes, sad things, thwarted lovers or dying.

For Elena Alvarado who could not hear

the music unless she went out to the patio, this particular day's end was a time of anger and despair. There were no children. In fact her nearest blood-kin were a thousand miles away in New York. If they had been closer it would not have helped much.

She ate without an appetite and went to bathe in the afterthought-room her husband had built off their bedroom.

It was not entirely the loss of possibly as many as fifty head of good horses that bowed her spirit, it was the simple fact that ranching in the South Desert country was not an occupation for a woman.

Batista had never even hinted at such a thing, but she could feel how the other men felt, three or four in particular, the ones who had followed her husband in manhunts that had taken as long as three weeks.

She could not continue to manage, which she had done for four years now, from her house and her yard, because she was a woman in a land made for men; eventually marauders would know there would be no violent pursuit when they raided the Alvarado ranch. In time the herds her husband and his father before him had raised to perfection in horseflesh through selective breeding would vanish as this last band had vanished.

John Henderson from the bank over in Hidalgo had mentioned last year that he thought he had a buyer for Alvarado Ranch. She had not mentioned this to Batista, in whom she otherwise confided fairly regularly. Batista was a godsend to her husband and had been the same to her, but regardless of his tact she had felt rather than seen a slow change in him since her husband's passing. If she sold Alvarado Ranch at all, but especially to a *norteamericano*, it would break the old *mayordomo*'s heart.

And not just his. Most of the riders were sons of fathers who had also worked for the Alvarados. The ranch was their home; more, it was their entire world. They had been born in the *jacals*, had matured in the dust of the working corrals.

She was combing her hair before the long mirror of her dresser when sturdy Rosalind whose father had been a passing-through Texan came to the doorway and said, '*Señora*, two of the men are in the patio.' As Elena stopped brushing and turned, the fair-skinned but dark-eyed woman avoided her eyes. 'Epifanio Garcia and Jose Duarte.' She left those names hanging in the silence, turned without meeting Elena's gaze and went soundlessly back to her kitchen.

Elena went back to brushing for a long moment, then deliberately twisted her hair into a coil, arose to dress as she usually did, in a split-hide riding-skirt of doeskin softer

9

than cotton, a white blouse, stamped into her boots and went through the house.

The mesquite fragrance lingered after sundown, even after night arrived. The men on the patio, hats in hand, were a contrast. Epifanio was not tall but was nearly twice as broad as his taller, leaner, equally dark companion. Duarte's expression was less set and dogged than were the features of Pifas Garcia. In fact Jose Duarte seemed uncomfortable being there when she greeted them, then stood waiting. Perhaps, if it had been left to Jose Duarte not a word would have been spoken.

Pifas smiled showing even, very white teeth and dark eyes without a shred of matching emotion. '*Señora*, it is about the stolen horses,' he said, speaking firmly.

She nodded.

'They were some of our best using-animals. Ten or twelve of them were beautifully reined.'

She could have motioned them to benches, instead she stood facing them, meeting their stares without wavering. 'And you want to take the men and go after them.'

Epifanio surprised her with his answer. 'No, *Señora*. Those horses are gone. We could not even see their dust by now. What we want is to ask you to make a younger man *mayordomo* so that the next time there is a raid he can take the men and bring back the animals—and settle with the thieves.'

She groped for an appropriate reply and ended up by telling them she would think about their proposal. They had to be satisfied with that. They knew, and Elena knew, it had not been enough.

CHAPTER TWO

THE DECISION

Batista Moraga had been correct; the *bandoleros* had raided north and east of Hidalgo and the *gringo* stockmen over there had boiled out in wrathful pursuit as though they had been bees and someone had struck their hive with a stick.

But Batista had not anticipated the implications of this pursuit. He was out behind the barn at the network of working-corrals when a youngster came breathlessly running to gesture in excitement and call to the men inside the corral that a large band of horsemen was approaching from the east.

Ramon Cruz, who had just shaken out a loop to rope a large unbroken three-year-old stud colt, peered through dust, saw Batista coil his *riata*, drape it from a post and climb out of the corral to follow the child. Ramon

11

looked at the big colt, swore, coiled his lariat while walking toward the gate, and was still holding the coiled *riata* as he entered the barn where it was cool and shady.

Besides Batista there was Pifas Garcia and Jose Duarte standing in silence watching the distant riders. The child breathed a word into the silence. '*Bandoleros.*'

Batista shook his head, gave the child a gentle shove and told him to go find his mother.

Garcia had thought the same thing when he had first seen the dust even though it made no sense; border-jumpers rarely raided in broad daylight and even more rarely rode directly towards the yard of large ranches where there would be many men. At least not unless there were a great many of them, and the distant horsemen with the sun at their backs were not raising that much dust. Garcia loosened his stance as he said, '*Gringos.*'

Batista Moraga nodded slightly but said nothing. None of them did until the horsemen were within a half-mile of the yard, then they walked up to the doorless wide front opening of the barn and slouched there. Jose Duarte was rolling a brown-paper cigarette as he drily said, 'They back-tracked the raiders.' He lit up, trickled smoke and with the riders entering the big yard from the east, he also said, 'Foolish. The trail will lead towards the border, not over here.'

That was true. Batista strode out to the long tie-rack and leaned there as the horsemen crossed towards him. There were twelve of them, armed to the teeth, unsmiling, mostly unshaven, well mounted and weathered to a uniform bronze skin-tone. The man who approached Batista was John Burket, one of the first of the increasing number of *norteamericanos* who had bought land on the South Desert. He was tall, lanky, soft-spoken, greying and likable even to the dark natives who in varying degrees resented the influx of *gringos*.

Burket drew rein, rested gloved hands atop his saddlehorn, looked around the yard then smiled down at the *mayordomo*. 'Batista, good morning.'

Moraga smiled back. '*Buenos dias*,' he said, and waited.

The horsemen swung to the ground and stood with their horses. Batista recognised a few of them, ranch owners—*patróns*. The others were their riders; he had seen some of them over at Hidalgo or more distant Cibola but he did not know them.

John Burket glanced once towards the main-house then said, 'Border-jumpers raided hell out of us last night. As near as we can tell they got maybe a hundred horses.'

Batista told of their loss and shrugged. He had made his judgment: These men were out for blood. They were armed to get it and looked capable. 'They didn't come back over here, *jefe*. They would have gone arrow-straight for the border.'

Burket nodded. 'Yeah.' He, like the others, was a direct individual. 'The reason we came over here is to find out if Miz' Alvarado wants her horses back enough to give us a few riders.'

Pifas Garcia, until this moment leaning in barn-shade, now strode forward. He was not fond of *gringos*. 'Friend, by the time we can get saddled the horses will be down in Mexico. Maybe already being divided among the *pronunciados*.'

Burket's direct blue eyes went to Garcia, whom he had met before on the range, and lingered there. 'There's a revolution goin' on down there,' he said, and Pifas replied without tact, 'We know that.'

'Well,' said the soft-spoken man, 'that's why we need more riders.' He paused as though expecting Garcia to argue. When this did not happen he continued speaking. 'We got about forty men. They're mostly already ridin' south. Me'n these gents came over here to see if we could get a few more men, then we'll head southeast and meet the others. They got a wagon.'

Pifas's brows climbed. He and old Batista exchanged a look. Forty men was not a posse, it was a small army. And with a wagon

14

for supplies. Batista glanced in the direction of the fortress-like massive house with its red-tile roof and large patio. 'You can ask the *señora*,' he said as Pifas Garcia walked to the tie-rack and interrupted. 'We will get ready while you talk to her.' Avoiding the *mayordomo*'s gaze Pifas turned, jerked his head at Cruz and Duarte and went down into the barn.

John Burket watched them walk away, drifted his gaze back to the *mayordomo*, the equivalent of a ranch foreman, and smiled. 'Mad,' he murmured.

Batista shrugged again. 'We lost maybe fifty of our best horses.' He jutted his jaw in the direction of the main-house. 'You can tie your horses here if you wish.'

Burket looped the reins, glanced briefly at his companions then crossed the yard. Batista watched him go, straightened up and gestured in the direction of a big stone trough. The *gringo* riders dutifully removed bridles and led their animals to drink.

Batista approached the men down in the barn with fire in his eyes. He stopped in front of Pifas Garcia. 'You don't make this decision,' he said coldly.

Garcia looked at the older man almost contemptuously but said nothing as the other men led horses inside from the corrals out back. He took down his bridle from the saddle pole and started towards a horse.

15

Batista's sharp voice stopped him in mid-stride. 'Put the bridle back. We do nothing until *La Señora* agrees to let us go.'

Garcia came around on the balls of his feet, eyes flaming. In Spanish he said, 'You old idiot. If it is left to you there will be no horses, no ranch, nothing at all a year from now.'

Batista shuffled forward. Pifas's sneer was clear even in barn-shadows when the old man hit him so hard his head snapped. He collapsed in a heap, entangled in the bridle.

The other *vaqueros* were stunned. Garcia put the back of a hand to his mouth, saw the blood and without haste got both legs planted squarely and came upright with a knife in his right hand.

From the sunlighted doorway a calm voice said, 'Partner, you drop that knife or I'm goin' to blow your head off.'

The speaker was a red-headed, beard-stubbled faded man of less than average height. The gun in his hand was as steady as stone. When Garcia did not obey fast enough the short red-headed man cocked his gun.

Batista Moraga had hurt his right hand and was flexing it when he addressed the red-headed man. 'It's nothing, friend. It will be all right.'

The other man replied without taking his eyes off Pifas Garcia. 'Didn't look like nothin' to me, mister. Cowboy, you're one second away from hell. Drop that damned knife!'

Pifas dropped it, glared, turned on his heel and left the barn by the rear opening. The *gringo* sighed, holstered his gun and wagged his head. 'Mister,' he said to Batista, 'if you two ride with us you better grow eyes in the back of your head.' He walked away. Ramon Cruz and Jose Duarte relaxed as Batista Moraga picked up Garcia's knife, hefted it, brushed the honed edge and also left the barn by its rear doorway.

Duarte and Cruz exchanged a look, then tied the animals they had brought inside and found places to sit. They had no intention of bridling or saddling a horse until they were told to. Cruz looked towards the empty rear doorway and brushed his chest with his fingers. 'I made the same mistake yesterday,' he told Jose Duarte. 'He is old but...'

Jose laughed. He knew. He had seen the *mayordomo* react in anger several times.

Several of the *gringos* sauntered into the cool barn, found comfortable places to wait and said nothing. Their red-headed companion had told them of the interlude. He was not one of the men in the barn.

Epifanio Garcia was sitting on an old wooden bench outside a small *jacal*, hands clasped, eyes on the ground, mouth set in an uncompromising line when the knife came

17

end over end to land in the dust at his feet. He looked up. Batista smiled faintly. 'It was nothing,' he said in Spanish, then switched to English, which was becoming common in the South Desert country. It was an easy language to learn. It was also easy to speak. 'We will ride with them, Pifas. But the lady is the boss. You can't do what you want to do in something like this and you know it. If her husband was still alive you wouldn't have acted like that.'

Surly dark eyes came up. 'He isn't alive. Just you an' her.' Garcia sighed noisily, straightened on the bench and looked up. 'What I said back there is the truth. If she and you don't do anything we won't have no horses, no nothing at all but empty land in another year or two. Batista, I did it because I don't want that to happen. What will happen to everyone? Even the ranch. What will happen to it?'

Before answering Batista shuffled to the shaded bench and sat down. He leaned forward looking at the ground. 'Don't you think I know these things? I know them as well as you do. But we work for her, she gives the orders.'

Pifas made an angry gesture with powerful arms. 'And loses everything, which means we lose too—everything.'

Batista was quiet for a moment. 'Listen to me,' he finally said. 'It is her ranch.'

18

Pifas turned to stare.

'I said it is her ranch. Do you know what will happen to you if you take the men and go after those bastards? She will fire you. Then you will have lost everything anyway.'

Garcia started to speak, checked himself, slammed his back against the mud wall and swore. Batista understood his frustration and smiled at it as he also leaned back. 'She don't need *pistoleros* any more than she needs a *mayordomo*. She needs a man. Alvarado Ranch needs a man. Pifas, I am old. I can tell you this much but not much more about life. If you know something should be changed and you know you can't change it, then you have to be patient and wait for it to be corrected by—someone anyway. God or someone.'

Garcia eyed the old man sceptically but remained silent. He had a streak of violence, a fierce temper, but a good heart. He had grown to manhood under the old *mayordomo*. The best of all that he had learned in the yard, at the corrals or fifty miles distant in horse-camps, he had learned from Batista Moraga. With a twinge of shame he picked up his knife, sheathed it and cleared his throat, lustily expectorated at a trail of tiny black ants and reached to lay a thick hand with blunt fingers on the older man's knee. Then he arose and went in search of an *olla*. He was thirsty.

Batista sat comfortably until he heard voices over in the vicinity of the barn, then shoved upright and walked towards them. He had recognised the voice of the woman he worked for.

Morning sunshine made her hair shine bluish-black. She was taller than the red-headed man standing with the other *gringos* as she and John Burket spoke. She had agreed that some of her riders could accompany Burket's band. She had also volunteered a wagon, which Burket had declined to accept, but he had suggested an alternative which she had agreed to. She would fill the saddlebags of every rider with enough food to last until they met the other riders somewhere southeasterly down near the border.

When she saw her *mayordomo* approaching she frowned a little. When he walked up she told him what had been agreed upon and asked him to select the *vaqueros* to ride with the *gringos*. He nodded. That would be no problem at all, unless of course she objected to him riding with them.

She asked him to name them, perhaps because she suspected something, so he named them first, and named himself last. She immediately shook her head at him. 'Someone has to be here, Batista. Besides...'

He looked straight into her eyes waiting

20

for what he knew she was going to say. She looked straight back, and reddened slightly. Lanky John Burket whom neither of them knew well, surprised them both with a demonstration of insight when he said, 'Ma'am, my paw was older'n him when he was still runnin' down renegades.'

Elena's gaze wavered.

Burket spoke again, and smiled at her as he did so. 'We're goin' to need every rider we can get who knows that border country. There's one thing I know about Mex border jumpers; they are *coyote*. They'll be watchin' for dust even after they're across the line, lady. If they see it, and sure as hell they're going to, they'll set up a bushwhack. That's why we need your foreman.'

Elena did not look at the lanky man, she looked at her *mayordomo*. Just before she nodded something her husband had once said came to mind. 'No matter what it is if it's trouble thank God for Moraga del Hidalgo.' She scowled at him. 'You be careful, Batista.'

He nodded and turned towards the barn where a large group of *vaqueros* were watching and waiting. There was going to be some injured feelings and some indignation because Batista did not intend to strip the ranch of men.

John Burket walked back towards the main-house beside the beautiful widow. As

21

they strolled he said, 'Now that it's settled, ma'am, I'll tell you what we plan.' He shot her a sidelong glance then studied the ancient carved wooden gates of the patio which they were approaching. 'We don't figure to stop.'

With a hand on the gate she stopped stone-still and looked at him. She thought she knew what he had meant. 'You are not going to stop?'

'At the border,' he replied meeting her gaze head on. 'Enough is enough. This here isn't goin' to be another ride to the line where everyone stops and down there the Mexicans watch and laugh. This time we expect to give them the surprise of their lives, and if we're lucky when we come back there won't be any more raids.'

She pulled in a shallow breath. 'You can't do that. It is against the law and the army will be waiting for you when you return.'

He smiled a little. 'Yes'm. If the army hears about it an' if the army can get over there fast enough. My idea is to ride down in there, get the horses if we can find them and if we can't to put the fear of Gawd into 'em. And do it all within one day. Two days at the most. Then get back up here before the army even hears about it.'

'Mister Burket, even if you succeed the law will still come after you.'

He shrugged wide shoulders. 'Miz'

Alvarado, the law hasn't done anything.
Neither has the army. You want to lose the
livestock you got left? Neither do we.
Ma'am, there just isn't any other way.' He
was turning when he also said, 'I'll look after
the old gent. I could tell he means a lot to
you.' He brushed the brim of his hat with a
gloved hand and strode away.

CHAPTER THREE

A COPPERDUST SUN

Batista had been right. When they left the
yard with laden saddlebags there was Jose
Duarte, Pifas Garcia, Ramon Cruz the
horse-breaker and Batista Moraga. Behind
them a sullen group of *vaqueros* stood rooted
in barn-shade watching Burket's band
pale-out under the climbing sun.

The slight, red-headed man whose cocked
gun had driven Pifas out of the barn offered
Batista a chew from his curl of
molasses-cured Kentucky twist. When
Batista declined the red-headed man gnawed
off a cud, pouched it into his cheek,
expectorated once, then stood in both
stirrups studying the flow of land as he said,
'My name is Travis Moore.' He settled down
on the saddle-seat still considering the miles

23

of emptiness which was beginning to acquire its customary heat-haze. He did not notice the sidelong look he got from Batista Moraga, who had never before met Travis Moore but had heard quite a little about him in the villages.

Pistolero. Gunfighter. *Muy matador.* A man who kills. Batista drifted his gaze forward where John Burket and another rider were in deep conversation, sometimes gesturing with gloved hands as they talked.

Travis Moore smiled. His smile was youthful, his size was only slightly more than child-like. Except under close scrutiny he looked young. He was past forty.

'That feller with the knife,' he said, paused to spray amber, then resumed speaking. 'He's trouble, partner.'

Batista smiled while wagging his head. 'No. I've known him since he was small. The *señora*'s husband hired him because he fears nothing and is deadly with guns—'

'He was goin' to cut you.'

Batista shrugged. 'He was angry, not at me but because night before last we lose maybe fifty of our best horses and he wanted to go after the raiders, not wait for the *señora* to think about it.'

Travis Moore slouched along for a short distance in pensive silence. When he spoke again it was not about Pifas Garcia. 'You know the border country?'

'I was born in Hidalgo. I know all this country.'

'How about down into Messico?'

Batista's dark eyes with their muddy whites became fixed on Travis Moore. 'For maybe a hundred miles down there. Why? Is that what John Burket plans; cross the line?'

Moore grinned. 'Well now, *mayordomo*, there was a pretty big pow-wow yesterday. What come out of it was that this here raiding's been goin' on for maybe ten, twenty years. That's a lot of lost livestock. I'm just a rider. Most of us are, but Mister Burket and the other owners got an idea it's got to end, even if we got to cross the border to end it.'

Batista continued to gaze at the shorter man. 'There is war down there.'

'Well hell, partner, there's always some kind of damned foolishness goin' on down there, ain't there?'

Batista did not answer the question. He said, 'In Mexican revolutions everyone is armed. Even the goat-herders. And there are armies. Sometimes with cannons, but always with hundreds of armed men. Some on foot, some on horseback. Usually half-full of *pulque* or *tequila*. Do you know what those people do when they are fighting each other and *gringos* appear? They stop fighting each other and all go after the *gringos*.'

Travis Moore was grinning again. He said,

'Partner, I grew up in Texas. When I was a button an' them Mex route-armies sashayed close to the border, raided over it now an' again, you know what my folks and all the other folks did? They made up a Texas army, went down into Messico and cleaned ploughs until you could shoot a cannon down the main street of their towns and not hit anybody at all.'

Batista nodded. He had heard of those campaigns. But then had come the big war between the *gringos* of the North and South. The South had lost and ever since the North had been patrolling not just the defeated Confederacy but also the adjacent Southwest.

He said, 'What about the border patrols and the army camps?'

Moore's grin turned crafty. 'The way Mister Burket an' the others got it figured, we'll track them horsethieves to the line, then set down an' wait until someone like you scouts around down there an' finds the horses. Then we'll cross over in the night, an' come dawn we'll hit those *pronunciados* or whoever's got our livestock, like a whirlwind, get as many of our horses as we can and ride like hell back up over the line.'

Batista put a squinted look over his shoulder where Pifas and Ramon were riding on each side of Jose Duarte, faced forwards and saw John Burket beginning to alter

26

course slightly, on a southward angle. Finally, he said, 'Well, we want the horses back, but friend, some of us may not come back.'

Travis Moore spat aside, ran a limp cuff across his chin and while considering the angle of their course, he said, 'It don't matter where you are or what you're doin', partner. When your time comes ...' He winked at Batista and reined away to ride forward.

They had to pick up the gait, heat or no heat, so they did it in the best way experienced desert horsemen knew to cover ground without exhausting horses; they loped for a mile or two, then walked for a mile or two.

They raised dust, which was unavoidable. The last time it had rained was early springtime, but even Batista doubted there would be any watchers on the marauders' back trail who would see it. Not two days after the raid.

They paused for a half-hour at the topless adobe hut of a long-dead old man. No one even remembered his name. He'd had a small band of goats. Indians had killed him, fired his house, of which only the faggot roof would burn, and because his goats could not keep up with their horses, they had also shot them and carried a few slung over the withers of their mounts as they raced away.

The same two things that had encouraged

the old man to settle down here in the middle of nowhere was what prompted John Burket's riders to pause there. Broad shade from several old unkempt cottonwood trees, and water which came coldly out of the earth to be held in a low, circular stone trough the old man had built. It was fresh, cold and sweet; anyone familiar with this part of the South Desert country knew where the spring was, as did animals who left their tracks in the sodden earth where water overflowed the trough. Among the natives it was called 'goat spring'.

A lanky, darkly tanned man with pale blue eyes, a cud in his cheek, and roping-gloves folded over his shellbelt, came over where Batista was sitting in shade chewing jerky, squatted without speaking, and watched the horses being tanked up for a while before saying, 'Charley Dawes. You're Batista Moraga. I knew your *patrón* real well. Fine man an' a decent neighbour.' Charley Dawes shifted his cud and still without looking at Batista, he also said, 'I been in this country a long time. Sometimes a man learns an' sometimes he don't. What I've learned is that the Messicans around Cibola an' Hidalgo got a sort of *huaracha* telegraph with the Messicans down over the border.' Dawes turned his pale eyes towards the *mayordomo*. The gaze was not unfriendly, it was speculative.

Batista understood. 'If you rode through the towns, everyone will have noticed your wagon and guns. Maybe someone would ride down there and warn the raiders. But I don't think so. The Mexicans up here have suffered more than you have from those men. For many more years.'

Charley Dawes seemed to be turning this over in his mind. He evidently was one of those people who thought a long time before arriving at a decision or placing blame. He pushed up to his feet because over by the trough other men were bridling and cinching up. 'All the same it might be a good idea to put some skirmishers out.'

Dawes strode away and Batista also got to his feet. Jerky allayed hunger but because it was cured with salt and pepper it made a man thirsty. He too went over to the trough where men were filling canteens as well as their bellies.

Pifas walked up to drink deeply and afterwards to grin wolfishly at the *mayordomo*. He was obviously pleased about being part of this strongly armed band of vengeance-seekers. He leaned close and said, 'You know what a Gatling gun is, Batista?'

Moraga knew although he had never seen one. 'Yes.'

'Well, that's what they have in their wagon. A Gatling gun along with blankets, food and ammunition.'

29

Ramon whistled. Pifas walked towards the waiting horses leaving the *mayordomo* looking after him. A Gatling gun? They killed people by the dozen. He saw John Burket mount up and went after his own animal. As he joined the others riding directly southward now, over a two-day-old broad trail of dusted-over horse-tracks, most of which had been made by barefoot animals, perhaps only about fifteen or twenty by shod horses, misgivings troubled him. As he slouched along watching the leaders up ahead, he decided Travis Moore had been right. This time the plundered stockmen were going to make an impression below the border which would not be forgotten for a long time.

He heard Pifas laughing and looked around. Handsome, fair and youthful Ramon Cruz had said something amusing. But Garcia's laughter sounded more like exultation than amusement to the *mayordomo*.

They walked for two miles. No horseman pushed a horse with a bellyful of water. The sun was canting to one side. The dust rose again. Heat seemed less than it had been. This was autumn, meaning that although the sun continued to bear down every day from a faded blue sky, it was losing some of its later-day heat, which was a blessing.

Evidently Charley Dawes had won acceptance of his idea of scouts out ahead because there was broad width of separation between four or five riders up ahead, sashaying back and forth through the thornpin and other coarse brush, little of which could not be seen over by a mounted man.

Those outriders started up four antelope who raced away faster than a horse could run. Another time, along towards late afternoon, someone out front hauled back and drew his handgun. Before he could fire at a coiled rattler in front, someone yelled at him not to shoot; the noise would carry too far, so the angry rider swung off, scouted up some rocks and stoned the snake to death.

The sun was rusty-red and sinking, their dust had a tawny tint, and agreeably, the daylong heat which had been diminishing as afternoon wore along became pleasantly less.

An odd combination rode together a couple of hundred yards ahead of Batista Moraga: Travis Moore, the diminutive Texan who had cocked his gun at Pifas Garcia this same morning, and Epifanio Garcia. They were slouching along in casual conversation as though they were old friends.

Batista fished in a saddlebag for another warped and shrivelled stick of jerky. He chewed methodically. Not only was jerky tough and leathery, unless it was thoroughly chewed it did not go down well.

Shortly before the sun left one of the

vedettes came loping back to confer with the men up front, around John Burket. Everyone watched, not especially wary but certainly curious.

When the outrider loped back the way he had come to take position in the line of scouts, John Burket turned back to ride down the column to Batista Moraga where he reined in and rode a yard or two in silence before saying, 'Dust. Maybe three, four miles ahead. What's down there; any goat camps or mud villages?'

There was nothing between their present location and the Mexican border except dusty underbrush, wide areas where even underbrush would not grow, rocks, maybe rattlesnakes and certainly plenty of ticks. He shook his head. 'Empty country from here to the border, and for miles down into Mexico ... Which way is the dust moving? Towards us or away from us?'

Burket tightly smiled. 'Either way it wouldn't be good, would it? If it's towards us and it's a band of raiders, we're goin' to have to stop 'em if we can. Away from us likely means they've seen us and are headin' down over the line to warn everyone and set up an ambush ... It's comin' towards us.'

Batista stood in his stirrups. The dust was faintly visible. Out where the scouts were riding it would be more noticeable.

He sat back down. 'Raiders, *jefe*. It's a long

32

ride from where they came from up to the Hidalgo and Cibola countries. They'd leave Mexico maybe in mid-afternoon so as to get up among the ranches in the dark.'

Burket nodded, having already arrived at this same conclusion. He rode with narrowed eyes, gloved hands resting atop his saddlehorn. 'If we've seen their dust sure as hell they've seen ours.'

Batista gazed at the other man's slightly hawkish profile. 'They've come farther than we have.'

Burket turned his head.

'They are hard on horses. They're probably half-drunk too. We can run straight at them and catch some before the others turn and race back.'

Charley Dawes joined them, his adam's-apple working as he chewed, his deeply lined, sun-dried dark face composed. 'Raiders,' he stated. 'Sure as Gawd made green apples. John, we got a good edge on 'em if you're of a mind to make a horse-race out of it.'

Burket nodded slowly. 'Once a cavalryman always a cavalryman, eh Charley?'

Dawes showed stained teeth in a smile. 'Yeah, I expect so. You want to charge them?'

Burket stood in his stirrups to study the dust. As he did this he said, 'I thought sure

33

we'd run into the others an' the wagon by now.'

Dawes spat aside before speaking. 'Ain't been any tyre-tracks since shortly after we got in below Hidalgo. I'd say they're maybe eastward somewhere. It'd sure help if they was close enough to see that dust too.'

The same outrider was loping back again. Burket reined away to ride ahead and meet him. As Charley Dawes rode beside Batista Moraga, he chuckled, turned perfectly calm eyes on the *mayordomo* and asked a question: 'You ever been in a horse battle?' Without awaiting an answer Dawes waved his arms. 'Everyone's goin' every which way, hollerin' and shooting. I been in a lot of them in the army an' I can tell you one thing, except for the noise an' dust an' sweat an' all, darned few men ever get killed. Usin' guns off the back of a half-crazy horse isn't no way to win a fight. You got to get off, and afterwards hope to hell you can find the horse.'

Burket was standing in his stirrups up ahead with a gloved hand raised overhead. The straggling band of horsemen halted. Burket turned back to continue his discussion with the scout, everyone else sat there watching and waiting. There was a ripple of talk, mostly subdued.

Charley Dawes rode towards the front, up where John Burket was turning back. Batista swung to the ground to squat in

34

horse-shadow and chew jerky, black eyes missing nothing. Jose Duarte walked up leading his animal and also squatted. 'What are they going to do?' he asked, and got back a cryptic answer. *'Yo no se.'*

Jose remained silent. If Batista did not know after riding with John Burket, then who would know? But he said nothing. Not until he suddenly stiffened and got upright. 'Did you hear it?' he asked.

Batista had heard nothing. Evidently Jose was not the only one who had heard something. The outriders were coming back in a lope. Visibility was still good and would remain so for several hours yet, even though the sun was gone and shadows had spread around the stands of underbrush.

Men were dismounting up ahead. A few had pulled Winchesters from saddle-boots. Everyone was peering dead ahead.

When Batista finally stood up Jose brushed him with a hand. 'Now do you hear it?'

Batista cocked his head, concentrated, then had to admit that he heard nothing.

Jose was moving away as he said irritably, 'Gunfire. Are you deaf?'

Finally, Batista heard it; a rattle of uneven shooting somewhere far ahead. Probably a couple of miles ahead.

CHAPTER FOUR

SIMPLE STRATEGY

There was dust but now it did not appear to be moving. Burket waved Batista Moraga forward. When they met he said, 'Take a man an' scout down there. Be real careful. If it's *rurales* or someone else from below the line chasin' another bunch from down there, we'll go back a ways an' keep out of it. This here isn't an army an' we're not soldiers.'

Batista took Jose Duarte and got a venomous look from Pifas Garcia for making that choice, but Batista wanted a careful man, not a fierce one.

They picked their way in and out of brushstands, raised practically no dust, which was not very noticeable anyway without direct sunlight to brighten it.

Duarte was the best tracker on Alvarado Ranch, but his ability was not needed now, not even when they had covered a mile and could hear gunfire very clearly. There were no tracks.

But there was dust and distant noise. Batista told Jose Duarte what Burket had said about Mexicans chasing other Mexicans and Jose shrugged and kept silent. He was devoting full attention to what they were getting steadily closer to: a battle of some kind.

The gunfire had been constant for about a half-hour. Now it was sporadic but it did not sound as though there were fewer shooters. There was probably less ammunition.

Batista halted behind a flourishing, tall thicket, dismounted, made his horse fast and lifted down his carbine. Duarte did the same. They stood together listening for a long while before Batista raised his Winchester and led off like an Indian, moving always in shadows, shade or beside clumps of brush.

When he saw where the dust was rising thickly he put out an arm to stop the man behind him, held his saddlegun in the crook of one arm and, as Jose stepped up beside him, Batista made a wide gesture.

'*Rurales!*'

Their short, red jackets were visible through the dust. They had been caught in a way that made Batista wag his head. Red-flaggers were the experienced and deadly brotherhood of killers in rural Mexico. They had the right to pass judgment and shoot at the same time. They were feared above all uniformed units in the country. They carried a red flag, signifying no quarter. They were thoroughly hated. What Moraga and Duarte saw was perhaps as many as fifty or sixty ragged *campesinos*, probably *pronunciados*, in a ragged circle with the *rurales* inside. Batista said, 'Ambush. It had to be. It's hard to believe. They never ride without scouts in all directions.'

Jose Duarte shrugged, his face expressionless as he watched the ragged *bandoleros* shooting, moving, hooting and taunting the besieged red-flaggers. No one liked *rurales*. He leaned to be heard over the noise and said, 'Let's go back. This won't last much longer. They can't break out. There are no more than fifteen or twenty of them.' He shrugged again to make it clear that if all the *rurales* were killed he would not shed a single tear.

Batista, who had no more feeling for the fiercely fighting men inside the rebel surround, was wondering about something else. 'They must have been riding north when they blundered into the ambush. Why? Do you suppose it was *rurales* who stole our horses?'

Duarte doubted that. *Rurales* did not have to raid over the line for saddle-stock. When they entered a village it was their custom to have every horse led out so that they could confiscate the ones they wanted. 'More likely,' he told Moraga, 'they were trailing the *bandoleros*, who were coming up into our country for horses.' Duarte turned to walk back to his horse.

Batista followed him with a furrowed brow. They said little on the lope back.

When they met Burket and the others, they dismounted to relate what they had seen and what they had deduced. Burket turned to Charley Dawes and several other men. Counting the four riders from Alvarado Ranch John Burket had sixteen riders. What was bothering him was the twelve men with the wagon of which there had been no sign yet.

He said, 'To go around them we'd have to ride east or west a lot of miles. Even then they might find our tracks.' He scowled. 'Where is the damned wagon?'

The former Confederate cavalryman was skiving off a cud with a wicked-bladed boot-knife and did not look up as he said, 'It wouldn't matter which way we went to get around 'em, gents. If they massacre them red-flaggers it'll make 'em more set on raidin' the country behind us. If they got likker along, an' sure as hell they have because they don't never seem to raid or fight without it, they're going to maybe hit Hidalgo or Cibola tonight. Maybe more ranches, where most of us had ought to be an' ain't.'

Dawes settled his cud and looked from face to face, dead calm and pensive. 'Sure never figured I'd ever say anythin' like this, boys, but without the others an' the wagon, there ain't enough of us to stop them raggedy-pantsed bastards. We better ride down an' rescue them *rurales*. With their guns an' ours I don't care if there's a hunnert of them raiders, we could sure stop 'em in their tracks.'

No one responded. Jose Duarte eyed the former horse-soldier with disgust but said nothing. Several of the nearby slouching riders muttered a little, looked southward where the gunfire seemed to be diminishing finally, and turned back as one man said, 'Charley's right. It's the last thing I ever figured I'd do, rescue them murderers, but he's right. What we're down here to do is clean out border-jumpers. This is a good chance to do it, and with them on our side of the line.'

There was muted agreement. It was not unanimous but when Burket, Dawes and several other men turned towards their horses, everyone else did the same.

Batista and Jose Duarte rode ahead with the scouts. They followed their own tracks. The gunfire now was accompanied by long intervals of quiet. The dust, less visible now as the long day was entering its final stage, was strong enough to be picked up by scent.

John Burket came up to ride with Moraga. When the *mayordomo* said they were getting close, Burket nodded without looking around at the speaker.

During those lulls in the fighting taunting catcalls in border-Spanish were audible as the stockmen sought places to tether their animals. Pifas Garcia shuffled up to Batista with his carbine draped loosely over one shoulder. He did not mention feeling slighted at not having been picked to be a scout. He watched Moraga take down his saddlegun and grinned. 'I'm a poor shot after sundown,' he said, black eyes bright.

Batista watched the others trudging back from tying their animals as he said, 'I know better. I've seen you shoot in this kind of light.' He slowly faced Garcia. 'I don't like them any more than you do, but remember, this one time we need them on our side. Don't shoot at them.'

Pifas gazed steadily at the older man, still smiling. He liked Batista Moraga, always had. He also respected him. But sometimes it made him uncomfortable to have his mind read.

Burket was talking to Charley Dawes a few yards away. Dawes was gesturing as he spoke. When he lowered his arm John Burket waved all the men up close and told them he would lead half and Charley would take the other half. Each party would keep to shelter and try to get around the *bandoleros*. Whether they would be totally successful or not, the moment they were seen, they were to fight.

The idea was to divert the attention of the attackers from the surrounded *rurales*, to confuse the attackers and to keep up a withering fire at them.

It was not brilliant. It was not even likely to succeed against larger numbers except that the *bandoleros* had been so exultantly confident they had not put out vedettes. Surprise was what John Burket was counting on.

The men from Alvarado Ranch went southeastward with Charley Dawes, whose rhythmic jaw movement did not increase at all as he alternately watched the men behind and around him, and looked for *bandoleros*. They found three, all dead. By the time it was possible to detect illusive movement beyond and out through the underbrush, the firing was picking up again. It seemed that the desperate red-flaggers were resigned to making their last fight.

The *bandoleros* were keeping up that derisive hooting and were now also yelling insults.

Charley Dawes held up his left arm, held it aloft for a long moment, then brought it down as an abrupt rattle of gunfire sounded northward of the *rurales* out through the dense underbrush. For five seconds not a shot was fired among the Mexicans. Even the shouting stopped.

Charley Dawes spat out his cud and raised his voice to say, 'Keep to cover, boys. Get belly-down if you got to. Let's go.'

This time the irregular firing came from the east, behind the *bandoleros* who had been tightening their surround as the red-flaggers fired less.

Dawes was about forty feet from Batista Moraga when he tilted his head and made a blood-curdling Rebel yell, then plunged ahead firing his Winchester from the waist holding it in both hands.

The *bandoleros* began to crumple. Those who recovered first from their astonishment ran like deer in all directions. A few sank to one knee to fire eastward and northward. The besieged *rurales* shot them in the back.

The men who had exulted over the success of their ambush were now the ambushed. They could not hold their ground under gunfire from three directions. Those still able to flee did so. When several of Charley's men would have gone in pursuit he profanely ordered them back and still turned the air blue after they had returned. One of them had been Pifas Garcia, but as he halted beside Batista, panting for breath, he watched the tall Confederate with obvious respect. With the noise dwindling he said, '*Muy soldado*,' and Batista nodded agreement. Charley Dawes was an experienced soldier.

The taste of dust was strong. Lingering daylight smelled of gunsmoke and sweat. John Burket's voice rose clearly from the northwest.

'*Rurales*; who is in command stand up.'

No one did so, but a tired man called back in English, 'I am Sergeant Escobar. The officer is dead. So is the man next under him in rank.'

Burket's reply carried all the way over to where Charley's men were waiting. 'I'm John Burket. The men with me are from ranches up north. Do you want to talk, Sergeant Escobar?'

Among the sweat-grimed, dusted-over embattled *rurales* someone laughed. The voice was different this time, the words were in Spanish. 'Everyone can talk. I want water.'

A stocky Mexican in a torn, filthy short red jacket stood up in the wreckage of dead animals and riddled *alforjas*. 'Escobar,' he called, and waited until John Burket appeared, then started ahead with his carbine in the bend of one arm.

There was not a sound until diminutive Travis Moore spoke quietly from behind Batista Moraga. 'They don't trust no one.'

Pifas drily answered, 'They got no reason to, an' when they get back to Mexico not a one of 'em will tell the truth—that they was saved by us. They'll make up a big heroic story about fightin' off a whole army of *pronunciados*, killin' half and scatterin' the rest like birds.'

44

Charley Dawes turned slowly, eyed Pifas, and laughed.

While the palaver was taking place in the middle distance Charley's men began to sidle around through the underbrush looking for whatever they could find.

Dead *bandoleros* were widely scattered. Aside from weapons, generally too badly abused to be worth taking, there were some beautiful silver-inlaid Chihuahua spurs, some money, both Mex and US, gold crucifixes, probably taken from murdered priests, and jewelery that had come from north of the border.

Burket called to Charley Dawes to approach the area of the surround. Batista and Ramon Cruz walked together. The youthful horse-breaker did not speak. There were dead men in the open, more half hidden by undergrowth. Cruz seemed not to see them.

The surviving *rurales*, some wounded, were moving in their circle. Only three or four walked out where Sergeant Escobar and the stockmen from up north were talking. Batista heard one man speak in Spanish to a companion. He sounded surprised as he said, 'But it sounded like a hundred of them. Look you, there is not even half that many.'

Escobar was sweat-drenched and drank repeatedly from canteens Burket's riders offered. He had trouble expressing gratitude

45

but made a strong effort to make it sound sincere when he thanked the *gringos*. He was certainly relieved. But for the *gringo* stockmen he would have been killed, but it was clear that Sergeant Escobar did not like *norteamericanos*.

CHAPTER FIVE

MEN WITH DOUBTS

There had been eighteen *rurales*. Nine had survived. Five of those nine were wounded.

As Sergeant Escobar told it, his party had picked up sign of insurrectionists heading for the border in the afternoon. His contingent had followed. At the border their captain had not even grunted. He kept on riding. Clearly, he had crossed the line before.

Neither Escobar nor any of his surviving companions knew how they had been ambushed, but one man, his short jacket over his shoulder, his body bandaged and one arm showing red through more cloth on his upper left arm, who looked old for a *rurale*, but might not actually have been old, had something to say.

In contrast to Sergeant Escobar this man smiled a lot and seemed not to dislike *gringos*. He told Batista in Spanish their dead officer had ignored the possibility of an ambush even though his lieutenant, also now dead, had warned him of the possibility. Sergeant Escobar listened stonily and gave the wounded man a bleak look.

It was hard work for nine men, all but four wounded, to dig graves for the dead. Burket's riders would not have offered to help if the men from Alvarado Ranch had not volunteered to dig, then three others went back to the battleground while John Burket sent Charley Dawes with four men to scout for the wagon.

Dawes led off his riders with dusk settling fast. For the others there was no laughter as the men made supper, the best part of which came from the bullet-ridden *alforjas* of the *rurales*. Miraculously, three bottles of pulque had not been broken. These were passed around but they did not improve the mood of the battered red-flaggers, who had lost companions. Burket's riders were weary from riding. Some of them put down ground-cloths, covered themselves with a single blanket, and slept. But generally, it was not a camp of men seeking slumber. Sergeant Escobar sat hunched by a tiny smokeless mesquite fire, occasionally speaking but for the most part solemnly silent. He refused the bottles which were being passed from hand to hand.

One of the wounded *rurales* went out of his

head close to midnight and alternately groaned and spoke in rapid Spanish. It was unlikely he would survive until morning.

Burket questioned Escobar. The sergeant knew of horse-raids. He had in fact seen a large remuda of stolen *gringo* horses the day before, down near a village called Dolores. Escobar raised coal-black eyes questioningly. 'You were going down there?'

Burket's retort was sharp. 'You're up here aren't you?'

Escobar continued to gaze at the rancher through a long silence, then went back to morosely gazing into the little fire. Finally, he said, 'There is a *gringo* soldier-patrol to the west. It is riding west. Maybe they heard the gunfire. Maybe not. If they heard it they will be coming back. If they find out you invaded Mexico they will arrest you.'

Burket nodded. 'I expect so. But we want those horses back. An' we'd like to put a crimp into the men who stole them.'

Escobar's dark eyes came up again. 'If you kill Mexicans in their own country when you are not supposed to be down there, maybe we would go to war with the United States.'

Someone loudly snorted. Several of the other men made similar sounds of derision. Escobar's dark eyes became ice-cold as he looked around at the *gringos*. When any of them would have wagered a year's pay he was going to show anger, he said, 'It can be done. Get your horses back.'

That older-seeming, wounded red-flagger nodded vigorously. He addressed his sergeant in Spanish. 'Those pronouncers will be down there. What's left of them.'

Escobar dropped his head in thought. The older rider spoke again. 'Getting their horses back can be done; we owe them that much.'

Escobar nodded without looking up. 'Even if they are *norteamericanos*. I would like some water then to sleep until sunup.'

After he had arisen and walked back into the shifting shadows of falling night, his friend, the man with two bandaged wounds, leaned a little and looked straight at Burket as he spoke again still in Spanish. 'His brother was among those killed. He owes you a debt so he will help you get your horses back.'

When the wounded *rurale* also went in search of a place to bed down, John Burket left the fire in the opposite direction. As he passed the place where the riders from Alvarado Ranch were lying, a quiet voice stopped him in his tracks.

'*Jefe*, don't rely on what they told you. Maybe they'll help you get the horses back. If someone in that town he spoke about, the one called Dolores, finds out *rurales* are helping *gringos*, no matter who wins their revolution, someone will come back to shoot those *rurales*.'

Burket squatted beside the speaker. 'Ambush, Batista?'

'Yes, I think so. There are too many of us for them to face in an open fight. Dolores is nothing more than a village. By now, with the war in that area, most of the people will be gone. The *rurales* who survived this fight can regain their honour by wiping out a big party of *gringos* who are invading Mexico.' Moraga showed white teeth in the night. 'They will never tell the truth about what happened up here today. I watched that sergeant; he hates *gringos*. He will make up a big story about being attacked by us and chased down over the line, and how he fought us to a standstill and shot the survivors.'

Burket pursed his lips, squatted in thoughtful silence for a long moment, then, as he leaned to arise he slapped Batista Moraga roughly on the shoulder before walking away.

An hour before sunrise while the early-risers were making little cooking-fires, Charley Dawes returned on a tired horse. His companions looked haggard. They said nothing until after their animals had been cared for, and they'd had black coffee.

One of them, a man named Rush Givens, had accompanied them from the wagon-camp, which had been fifteen miles to the south and west.

John Burket took Givens and Dawes apart, and while the others were eating, including the *rurales*, he told them what Moraga had said. Dawes accepted it without question. The man from the wagon-camp scratched a beard-stubbled face and twisted to eye the Mexicans. As he turned back he said, 'Well now, gents, knowin' this might happen will sure help. While we been settin' down yonder waiting for you to show up, we done a little scouting. There was a hell of a battle not very far from Dolores. It ended with the army chasin' them *pronunciados* all over the country shootin' an' saberin' 'em. The army pulled out. I reckon what's left of them rebels snuck back into the village.' There was a pause as the man from the wagon-camp rolled and lit a cigarette. He looked out through fragrant smoke with a grin.

'I expect with a little figurin' we could reverse this idea of ambushin' folks. Mister Burket, we can go down to them little swales and low hills east of Dolores in the night, set up our gun in the bushes, and lie there until we see them *rurales* settin' up their ambush. I don't expect it'll make a lot of difference how many rebels snuck back into the village. Most Mexes hate *rurales* worse'n they hate the devil, or even *gringos*. You can come down from the north. When it's over maybe we'll have enough time to search for our livestock.'

51

Charley Dawes had listened with approval right up to the man's last statement, then wagged his head. 'We're goin' to be makin' a war, gents, an' I don't care how far that Mex route-army has gone, sure as hell it's goin' to hear the Gatling gun or someone will ride out and tell 'em who we are and what we're doing.'

Burket told Rush Givens to go back to his wagon-camp and get ready to move down into Mexico after nightfall. He told Charley Dawes as soon as the men had eaten, they would send the *rurales* down to find and corral their stolen livestock at the village of Dolores.

Rush Givens departed after eating, heading back the way he had come. Charley Dawes ate, mostly in silence, then went in search of a razor and some soap so that he could shave.

Departure of the red-flaggers was delayed for more than an hour while riders scoured the countryside for loose saddle-stock and fetched it back to the camp. During this interval Sergeant Escobar put forth the exact proposal Batista Moraga had guessed about last night: He and his surviving men would go down to Dolores and search for the stolen horses.

Burket listened to Escobar with his heart hardening towards the *rurale*. But he smiled, they shook hands, and as Burket went

52

elsewhere in the camp several *gringos* helped the injured Mexicans into the saddle, gave them jerky and watched them ride south.

When the only Mexicans left were the riders from Alvarado Ranch, John Burket assembled everyone and explained the plan.

There was no particular opposition but there were a number of questions and even a couple of woodtick-strategists who wanted to advance their own plan.

Burket had plenty of time. He had no intention of striking camp as long as those *rurales* might still be able to see him coming. He wanted them to believe he would not appear at Dolores until late the following day.

The men cared for their animals, taking particular care to make certain shoes were tight, there were no galls, that the beasts were rested. Water was a problem; each man had to lead his horse a mile to a sump-spring and a mile back. They also returned with full canteens.

There was a lot of palavering, but by early afternoon the men were becoming restless. That there was considerable heat without a cloud all the way to the horizon added to the restlessness.

Of John Burket's sixteen riders less than half did not have some private plan of their own to submit for Burket's consideration. By the time the position of the sun let Burket know it was time to strike camp and ride south, he had been hoping this would happen for at least two hours.

Once in the saddle and moving, there was a lot less talk. Batista and Jose Duarte rode for at least two miles, side by side, without so much as a grunt passing between them. Up ahead where Pifas Garcia and the Texas gunman Travis Moore rode together the talk was sporadic.

Burket and Dawes rode in the lead. Beyond them several outriders scouted the onward countryside.

Duarte suddenly said, 'Batista, there is a lot of risk.'

The older man gravely inclined his head. 'Any time men ride like this there is risk. And there are deaths.' He considered the solemn profile of his companion and smiled to himself. Before the danger arrives, men can't say enough about what they would do if they could find horsethieves. When they are getting closer to the outlaws, they say very little.

When Jose made another remark, Moraga was ready with an answer. 'If there was a Mexican route-army in Dolores, when they rode away they would have taken our horses, if they were ever in Dolores.'

Batista nodded about that too, then he said, 'Do you want to go back, Jose? No one will stop you.'

Duarte reddened, reined out to let most of the column go past, and fell in at the rear of the column to ride stirrup with Ramon Cruz.

One of the cowboys pushed up to take Duarte's place and grinned over at Batista. 'If that Mex army don't turn around and come back, an' if no US soldier-patrol hears the racket and comes back too, I figure we've got a decent chance—if the horses are there. You expect they are down there?'

Batista did not know where the horses were. He told the cowboy not to feel badly if they never saw those horses again.

A scout rode back towards the head of the line in a nice little gathered lope which made Batista suspect that whatever he had to report, it was not very critical or he would have come back at something faster than a collected lope.

Word filtered back towards the rear of the column that the scout had reported seeing dust far to the west. Everyone squinted off in that direction. Batista Moraga thought it was that yankee patrol returning after their prolonged westerly scout.

He kneed his animal up towards the head of the column to ask whether it might not be a good idea to have someone scout over in that direction for a few miles.

John Burket's eyes twinkled as he said, 'You can go, Batista. Just be very careful.'

This time there was no mention of a

companion but he got one anyway. A mile from the column, passing in and out among stands of thorny underbrush he heard a rider to the rear and reined to one side to watch as Jose Duarte came along, head lowered, studying Moraga's tracks.

Batista rode into sight and said, 'Did someone send you?'

They hadn't. 'No, but two sets of eyes are better than one set.'

They rode together for more than a mile, until they could see the rising dust fairly well, then sat atop a low, brushy knoll watching straggling soldiers in blue uniforms slouching along as though they had been in the saddle many hours.

Duarte blew out a relieved sigh. 'Too far southward.'

He was correct. Unless the army patrol halted for a couple of hours, which would permit Burket's riders to get down closer to the border, possibly even cross it leaving tracks the patrol would intercept, there was very little danger.

Moraga and Duarte turned back riding at a fast walk. Anything faster would have stirred high dust.

When they found the column, the men were resting in the shade of some huge corpse-grey rocks where they had located a piddling trickle of tepid water that smelled faintly of rotten eggs. Even thirsty horses did not drink eagerly nor very much and the men did not drink at all. They still had water in their canteens.

They listened to what Batista had to report and decided to remain where they were until the soldier-patrol had passed by on its eastward course. The distance was about a mile and a half.

Burket's order was for each man to assume responsibility for himself and his horse. No loud noise was to be permitted.

Pifas came over into stone-shade and squatted where Batista was dozing with his old hat tipped down to shield his eyes. Garcia said, 'There will be scouts sent down over the line in the dark. How far is the village of Dolores from the border?'

Batista replied without lifting his hat. 'Maybe six or eight miles.' He raised the hat to gaze at Garcia. 'And you want to be one of the scouts.'

Garcia spread his hands, palms down. 'We could go together.'

Batista shrugged. 'Yes. If the *jefe* don't have others in mind.'

Garcia arose and walked away. Batista held his hat up and watched Pifas heading for the shady place where several men including John Burket were sitting. Then he lowered the hat with a rattling sigh and closed his eyes.

CHAPTER SIX

BLOOD, DUST AND DEVASTATION

The patrol passed along raising very little dust, but to Burket's watching men it was enough.

Nothing was done for an hour after the soldiers had moved eastward; John Burket studied the position of the sun, as did others. By estimate they were less than two miles from the border. The village of Dolores would be another six or eight miles. It was not a very great distance and if they took their time they should be approaching the village towards sundown.

After a council it was decided to make a camp where they could watch the village, and to do a little scouting on foot to make certain they were safe from discovery and attack. Otherwise, to wait until dawn to move in closer.

When the subject of scouts to go in advance down into Mexico came up, John Burket nodded in the direction of Batista Moraga and Pifas Garcia.

They left while the other men were still enjoying the shade. Batista was not in a talkative mood. Pifas tried several times to get a conversation going, but after receiving little more than grunts, he rode in silence.

The country they passed through was rockier than the northerly areas had been. When they reached the border, which was marked by little piles of rocks painted white, Batista halted, wiped the inside sweatband of his hat, gazed in silence down into Mexico and finally spoke.

'Do you know what happens if they take you alive down there?'

Pifas knew. '*Ley fuga*?'

'Yes. Have you ever seen it done?'

'No.'

'I hope you never do. Come along.'

The countryside appeared to be empty. To a considerable degree it was; not exactly empty, but abandoned. Mexican battles were fought according to no rules except those concerned with killing. People, along with animals, were shot out of hand. Few things which could be destroyed were not, including churches, often packed with people relying on the inviolability of holy sanctuaries.

Batista and Pifas Garcia did not see signs of the devastation until they were several miles into Mexico. Then it was dead animals, horses, half starved cows, goats, even chickens. But they picked up the scent of battle even earlier, before they rode carefully through the low, largely barren hills which paralleled a dusty road heading crookedly for the village of Dolores.

Once, they saw a family *careta* being drawn by an emaciated horse moving surreptitiously eastwards through the same low hills. Otherwise they did not see a living soul until they distantly saw rooftops, left their horses in a hidden place, took their carbines and went ahead on foot.

The village was a shambles. What could be burned had been fired. Adobe buildings in the main thoroughfare of Dolores had been blown apart by either set-charges or cannonfire. Miraculously untouched was a limp white sheet hanging from a pole above the local *parroquia*. Below, a pair of shattered wooden doors lay in the dust. Around the doorless opening were pockmarks from rifle bullets, evidence that seeking protection inside the church had not saved lives.

Batista lay flat out in the slanting sunlight. Beside him Pifas Garcia used his left hand to signify the stations of the cross on his thick chest.

Batista grunted and jutted his jaw. A solitary figure moved into the church doorway smoking a thin cigar. The man was half in shadow but even at that distance the unique short red jacket was recognisable. Neither watcher said a word. The *rurale* moved out into sunlight, flicked ash, crossed the dusty roadway and disappeared inside another doorless adobe structure. It was the local *cantina*. It was likely that not all the bottles had been broken.

Batista made a guess that other *rurales* were in there, drinking where it was cool. Pifas nodded almost mechanically. He had seen many fights, had been involved in his share, but this was something he had never seen before; a town that had been very close to the centre of a genuine battle.

He murmured under his breath. Batista looked around, then turned his gaze back to the silent village. He was looking for corralled horses. There could have been some which were not visible from where they were lying, but Batista did not think so. Clever ambushers would have got horses somewhere and put them where they could be seen as bait for the *gringos*.

There was no requirement for *rurales* to be clever, only merciless. Batista rolled on to his side to gauge the time of day from the position of the sun. He thought Burket's riders would be moving by now.

He was preparing to slide backwards before arising when a mounted man entered the silent village from the southwest. He was not wearing the red jacket. He was not in any other kind of uniform either. Batista settled down to watch as the horseman walked nearly the full length of the roadway and stopped his horse near the church. He sat gazing in that direction for some time, until a *rurale* called from in front of the saloon, then the rider turned and the *rurale* twisted to call to someone inside the *cantina*. Two other red-flaggers emerged.

The horseman swung to the ground holding reins in his right hand and Batista groaned. He should have been holding the reins in his left hand which would have left his right hand free to use his weapon. Pifas tipped down his hat to squint hard before he said, '*Viejo*, it is a priest.'

Batista watched and said nothing as the *rurales* strolled towards the stranger. The distance was too great for any conversation to be heard by the prone watchers, but when a *rurale* laughed as he reached for the rider's animal, and the priest refused to relinquish his hold, they heard the laughter.

A *rurale* struck the priest with his gunbarrel. The blow missed the man's head and came down on his shoulder. The priest dropped his reins and tried to twist away before he was struck again. He also stepped clear. The second blow missed completely, the other *rurales* laughed, which seemed to enrage the man with the sixgun. He roared curses which carried perfectly to the watchers and lunged at the priest swinging his gunbarrel like a club.

The priest went to his knees. Pifas Garcia made an animal sound in his throat and gripped his carbine to spring to his feet.

Batista placed an iron fist over the gun, holding it to the ground. 'Be quiet. Lie still,' he commanded in Spanish. 'You fool. The gun will not shoot that far. You will get us both killed.'

Garcia remained taut as a bowstring but did not get to his feet.

The *rurales* got the priest to his feet. He staggered, his hat was in the dust, his coat was torn, he could not raise his head. Batista said, 'It won't take long. God be thanked he is stunned.'

The *rurales* led the unsteady priest to the centre of the roadway, pointed him southward and ordered him to run. He seemed too dazed to understand so they punched him, forced him to walk away from them in a staggering shamble.

Batista breathed two words. *'Ley fuga.'*

But it was not even that. Victims of *ley fuga* were given the chance to run for their lives. They almost never made it, not with a crowd of half-drunken men with rifles or carbines hooting and laughingly encouraging the victim to run faster. They ordinarily did not begin shooting until the victim was several hundred feet away.

The *rurales* shot the priest seven times while he was staggering in a daze.

The sound of that gunfire carried in all directions. While it was still echoing the redflaggers walked past the dying man and stamped back inside the *cantina*.

Batista rapped Garcia's rigid gun-arm and began pushing backwards to be out of sight of the village before he arose. On the way back to their horses he looked at Pifas and said, 'We can find a high place and wait. If they don't get down here until dark we'll have to locate them by sound.'

Pifas acted as though he had not heard. Batista shrugged and made no further attempt to get a conversation going. Instead he angled through the low hills looking for a place where Burket's riders could camp through the night.

What he settled for was a grassy swale with a sluggish warm-water creek at its bottom, and stumps where trees had once stood. It was not as close to higher ground as he would have liked but as he told Pifas while they were riding across it, it was God's custom to give people half of what they needed so that they would not expect convenience even though they might ask for it, or thought they deserved it.

He led the way northeastward towards the nearest top-out. By the time they got up there a light breeze was blowing to cool things. Also, from this point of vantage they could see thin dust rising up in the direction of the border, but miles eastwards.

It was not being made by Burket's party. They would not be so far to the east. Batista swore to himself, expecting either Mexican soldiers or *bandoleros*.

He left the top-out riding due northwards, satisfied that if he could not see the makers of that dust, they would be equally incapable of seeing two riders who made almost no dust.

Very slowly Pifas Garcia's outrage turned to bitter ash. With dusk near he finally spoke. First he cursed in a cold, almost inflectionless voice, then he swore he would exact payment for the priest. 'It will make his soul lighter,' he told Batista, who put a level, calm gaze across the little distance separating them, and said nothing.

It was no longer possible to see that easterly dust, but there was still fair visibility as Batista led off down a long slope to flat ground. It was now possible to lope the animals, so they did so, and an hour later they saw three horsemen fairly far from one another, and drew down to halt to watch them approach.

One of those horsemen was Jose Duarte. Another was the small gunman, Travis Moore. The third man was a rider Batista had seen among John Burket's party, but had never spoken to and had no idea what the man's name was.

Duarte came ahead by himself. The other two scouts sat and watched. Pifas raised a calloused hand in high salute. Duarte did the same, lifted his horse over into a lope and met them about a half a mile from the two scouts he had left behind. There was not much said except that they had seen the *rurales* and the village. Batista did not mention the murder. Pifas rode grimly quiet all the way back where the main party had stopped at sight of the scouts returning with Garcia and Moraga.

Pifas ignored Burket and Dawes, rode completely down the column and turned in beside Ramon Cruz to whom he told his story.

Up front the palaver was not prolonged. At everything Batista said Charley Dawes chewed slowly and nodded his head. John Burket gave the older man a slap on the shoulders and sent him to find something to eat.

They rode over the line and were heading straight for the village when Batista hurried ahead to show them the way to the camp he had found; the only place where there was water and grass, and they would be hidden.

Then he left by himself, still troubled about that banner of dust they had seen before dusk. The last thing he wanted to happen was for a band of *pronunciados* or Mexican soldiers to catch his friends down in that arroyo where the camp was, which he was certain they would attempt to do if they had any idea there was a war-party from north of the border invading Mexico.

He was still scouting in the near-darkness when Pifas told his story around a fireless camp, with Burket and the others neither moving nor making a sound. Charley Dawes seemed the least moved; he had seen death in just about every guise it wore. He was not without feeling, but neither was he able to become as enraged as Garcia was. If he had tried to analyse his mood, which he did not attempt, it would have been one of seasoned sadness, the same feeling he had felt many times before.

Normally, this close to a Mexican village with livestock in it, coyotes prowled and made their eerie cries. Tonight there was not a sound. There was not a coyote within miles of Dolores.

Batista Moraga was not conscious of the lack of coyote-calls after hearing metal grate over stone in the middle distance. He was, by rough guess, about four miles from the Burket camp.

He swung silently to the ground beside his horse and waited patiently for another sound. It was a long wait, and it was almost ruined by his horse, who had picked up the scent of other horses and was raising its head to whinny when a dark hand closed down like a vice over the animal's nostrils. The horse forgot about making a noise.

Batista called the horse an uncharitable

name in Spanish, and stood waiting. The next sound he heard was of harnessed horses being hauled back on their britchings as though whoever was behind them needed their weight to hold back a load.

Batista let go with a rattling long sigh, swung back into the saddle and headed directly towards the noise. He had proceeded less than fifty yards when four horsemen loomed in the dark, two on each side, all four pointing cocked sixguns at him.

He halted, let his hands lie in plain sight atop the saddlehorn, and said, 'My name is Moraga.'

One dark rider edged closer, eased down the hammer of his weapon, holstered it and turned to say, 'Batista Moraga, *mayordomo* of Alvarado Ranch.'

A tall Mexican rider came up for a close look, and smiled so wide his teeth shone white in the gloom. He spoke in Spanish, 'You crazy old one, you could have been shot. Why didn't you call out?'

'Because,' Batista explained, also in Spanish, 'how was I to know who you were? There are *rurales* in Dolores, and *bandoleros* elsewhere, and God alone knows what other enemies are in the night. Are you satisfied?'

They escorted him back where seven other men and a sweating teamster were waiting. The teamster was holding his hitch back on their britching. The wagon at his back was tipped downhill.

When he was reassured it was not a band of renegades or soldiers, he talked up his team, stood on the binders and tooled it carefully down to level ground. Then he looped the lines around the brake handle, climbed down, hurled his hat to the ground and swore for a full minute without once repeating himself.

He had had one of the worst scares of his life.

CHAPTER SEVEN

DEATH AND DARKNESS

One of the riders who had accompanied the wagon was a dark man named Esteven McCoy. He was one of those cross-breeds who were equally at home on both sides of the border, whose Spanish and English were accentless, and whose temperament was occasionally baffling but usually good-humoured. By daylight his eyes showed gunmetal-blue with dark flecks and his features were less coarse than the features of many dark Mexicans.

He knew every inch of the countryside around the village of Dolores because he had been born there about forty years earlier.

When John Burket was discussing their position with Batista Moraga, Esteven McCoy ambled up to squat and listen, then to agree with everything Batista told Burket except one thing. Esteven McCoy knew something Batista had no reason to know.

Wherever their Gatling gun was positioned there had to be something to anchor the wheels to, otherwise as the gun fired, recoil drove it backwards. And there was one other thing: the range of a Gatling gun was about the same as that of a long-barrelled rifle. It was not like a cannon whose charge would hit something two miles away.

Batista listened, scratched, chewed jerky and when McCoy had explained, he smiled at the younger man and spoke in Spanish. 'It is something rare to know about these guns, isn't it?'

The grey-eyed man grinned and replied in English. 'Might be. For me, I've seen them used over in Texas.'

Charley Dawes ambled up and squatted. For once his jaws were not moving. Burket told him what they had been discussing and Dawes looked at Batista Moraga. 'Is there a place down yonder where we can set up the gun?'

There were no trees, if that was what Dawes had had in mind, so Batista replied by saying that since they would make enough noise to raise the devil if they tried to get right up to the village, if they could dig holes to set the wheels in, he thought he could show them a good position. Then he also said, 'I only saw three *rurales* down there. If there are no more we wouldn't need the gun.'

Dawes made a statement that did not startle Burket nor McCoy but which certainly caught Batista's attention. 'There may be a lot more when we commence firin' down there.' He jerked his head. 'There's a big band of Mex lancers approachin' Dolores from the south.' At Moraga's round-eyed look, Charley Dawes pointed towards John Burket. 'He saw 'em before it got too dark with his brass spyglass.'

Batista felt a chill. While the others watched him he removed his old hat, raked bent fingers through his thick, coarse grey hair, then replaced the hat. Gazing at Burket he said, 'If you knew that before darkness last night, why did you come down here? Mexican route-armies put their lancers far ahead to sweep the countryside. If you saw very many of them, maybe a regiment, if you had had more daylight you would eventually also have seen an army coming.'

John Burket exchanged a glance with Charley Dawes before answering. 'Where are our horses?' he asked, and when Batista shook his head, Burket thinly smiled. 'Then we'll have to do a little horse-stealin' of our

71

own.'

Batista's eyes widened. 'Those lancers?'

Dawes was groping through his pockets for some Kentucky twist when he drawled a reply. 'Why not? If we can set up a decent ambush ...' He found the plug and paused long enough to worry off a corner of it. 'We got all night, Batista. Mister Burket don't figure those lancers to reach Dolores until late tomorrow morning.' Dawes turned discreetly aside to spray brown juice, then turned back, sunk-set eyes fixed on Moraga. 'Down here it happens every day. Up north we do it too, not as much nor as often as they do it down here. We sort of frown on ambushin' folks, but down here it's their way of life.'

'With how many men?' Batista asked, and got a reply from Esteven McCoy.

'What you see, friend.'

Batista did not have to look around. At the most John Burket's party, including the men who had brought the wagon, numbered slightly over thirty. If that was a regiment of lancers Burket had seen, it could be as many as two hundred men, but probably less because Mexican regiments rarely were at full muster, except in times of peace, which these were not.

But if there were only one hundred lancers it was still more than three times the number of men with John Burket.

McCoy grinned over at Batista Moraga. 'We have seventeen slides for the gun. Do you know how many bullets that is?'

Batista had no idea. He shook his head.

'Enough,' stated McCoy, 'to cut down a regiment of lancers like they was tall hay.'

Batista did not feel quite reassured. 'And when you cut them down the noise will bring the route-army on the run. Mexican route-armies can have as many as five to eight thousand men in them.'

Dawes said, 'We're not goin' to fight no battle. We're not goin' to fight those lancers if we can get our horses. If there isn't no fighting we'll head north with the horses before those lancers see our dust. In the early morning.'

Batista gazed from one man to the other and ended up staring at John Burket, then shook his head. 'There will be fighting. Those *rurales* in the village are waiting to ambush you. If we don't turn back right now, if we go into the village, there will be gunfire.'

Burket smiled straight at Moraga. 'Be nice if we could avoid a lot of shooting. Pifas Garcia has volunteered to take four or five men and sneak down into the village in the dark, catch those red-flaggers from behind and use knives on them.'

Batista was surprised again. He looked around but there was no sign of Garcia, nor, for that matter, Ramon Cruz or Jose Duarte.

John Burket spoke again. 'They're waitin' on the far side of the wagon. You can go with them or you can show us how to find a place to dig in the gun.'

Esteven McCoy was rolling a smoke as he said, 'I can show them where to emplace the gun if you want to go with your friends.'

Batista arose without another word and trudged in the direction of the wagon. It was a dark night with many stars but no moon. Not yet anyway.

His friends were sitting slightly apart from the other men. Only Jose Duarte was smoking. When Batista arrived, settled his back against a wagon wheel and sighed, the other three gazed at him. He said, 'They are going to put the gun as close to the village as they can. Esteven will show them where.' He turned his head slowly. 'Do you know there is a route-army coming from the south?'

They knew. Duarte was punching out his smoke when he replied. 'What I don't like is the waiting.'

That did not trouble Batista. 'The army will make camp. There is plenty of time. But with thirty men it is foolish to even think of fighting tomorrow.'

Pifas Garcia snorted. 'By morning we will be gone, maybe without our horses, but there will be another time.' He arose to dust his britches, shifted the hip-holster into its

74

correct position and looked around. The others got to their feet. A hundred feet away where some cowboys were loafing, someone laughed, otherwise except for an occasional stamping horse, there was very little noise.

Pifas gestured for Batista to take the lead. He trailed around behind the wagon and skirted even wider around the place where Burket, Dawes and the man with the gun-steel eyes were sitting, and did not slacken pace until they could dimly discern buildings. Normally, there would have been dogs barking. Not tonight.

Batista finally halted. They were on the east side of Dolores facing the back of five or six buildings aligned in a row. Pifas brushed the *mayordomo*'s arm and pointed. 'That will be the *cantina*,' he murmured, and leaned on his grounded Winchester studying that particular building.

On the far side of the bullet-pocked buildings a horse squealed and another horse squealed back. Evidently there was a corral back there. It had not been visible from the place where Moraga and Garcia had scouted up Dolores in daylight.

Batista shook his head. Two horses were little better than no horses. He started soundlessly towards the rear of the *cantina*, and stopped stone-still gesturing for his companions to squat as a thick, heavy man came around from the roadway to sidle

75

against the building. The man looked around, looked down, fidgeted a little and went back towards the roadway.

Ramon Cruz breathed a single word. '*Soldado!*'

Batista twisted around. 'Are you sure?'

Ramon replied sharply. 'Didn't you see the sabre-chain on his belt?'

They hadn't. Batista sat on his haunches. Garcia and Duarte also sat down. Ramon Cruz said, 'Wait. Give me time to get up where I can see better or maybe hear them talking.' He was gone in the darkness before the others could stop him.

After an interval of silence Jose Duarte spoke. 'If there are soldiers here—how many will it be? How close is the army?'

He got no answer. A flaming star seared the underbelly of heaven leaving a tailrace of white brilliance in its wake. Pifas continued to look upwards after the light was gone. Batista knew what Garcia was thinking: A falling star meant death. One with an intensely brilliant tail meant many deaths. He said, 'It can't be meant for us. We are only about thirty men.'

Garcia brought his head down slowly, and smiled. 'Soldiers. There are many soldiers.'

Ramon appeared as soundlessly as a wraith and startled Pifas. He squatted to gesture with one arm. 'Nine soldiers. They were scouting ahead of the lancers. They are in there with the *rurales* drinking and talking loudly.'

Pifas started to speak but the *remudero* waved him to silence. 'The corral behind the *parroquia* is full of horses.'

They stared at him. Nine mounted soldiers and maybe four or five *rurales* with horses did not add up to a corralful, it amounted to no more than thirteen or fourteen head. Duarte needed reassurance. Ramon gave it to him, gesturing again. 'I passed mounds of saddlery over there, flung in all directions. Even saddle-guns still in their boots.'

Pifas and Batista spoke almost simultaneously. 'The *rurales* ... After they left us they rounded up all the horses left over from their fight with the *bandoleros*. It couldn't be anything else.'

Batista reached inside his shirt to scratch. He got to his feet pointing back in the direction they had come from, and, speaking rapidly, told Ramon to go find the others, tell them not to unload the gun from the wagon, but to get mounted, send the wagon back north, and come to the village on the east side where the corral was.

Ramon ran. Duarte and Garcia watched Batista Moraga.

A tall Mexican who staggered a little and was hatless left the *cantina* by a rear door. He was smoking a thin cigar whose scarlet tip

77

glowed at intervals. The tall man headed for a small building no more than two hundred feet from where Batista and his companions had been standing, and were now lying flat on the ground. Pifas Garcia's breath ran out in a hiss. Batista too had recognised that *rurale*. He put a hand upon Garcia's arm. Pifas shook it off and started ahead. Batista took two steps in pursuit then halted. If they argued or perhaps even struggled, the man in the little building would hear them.

Batista flapped his arms and when Jose came up beside him, he said, 'If that *rurale* yells out it will ruin everything.'

Duarte was watching the little building very intently. Pifas Garcia was almost up to it, moving like a wraith. Duarte said, 'He is holding his knife.'

Moraga wanted to swear. A gunshot would bring men boiling out of the saloon. A knife, even if it went through the *rurale*, would not kill him before he could scream or yell out.

The night was silent except for an infrequent raised voice in the *cantina*. They could no longer see Pifas. Batista's nerves were crawling, his muscles were taut.

There was not a sound for a long while, then Pifas appeared behind the little house walking towards them as though he were enjoying the blemishless warm night. He halted in front of Batista and raised his arm.

Dull starlight shone off a rosary with ivory beads and a magnificently crafted crucifix.

Jose said, 'Did you hit him over the head first? He didn't yell.'

Garcia was pocketing the rosary when he replied. 'There is no noise but air coming out when you cut a man's throat.' He faced Batista. 'I know. I shouldn't have done it. It puts us all in danger.'

Moraga said nothing. He jerked his head to lead the way southward among the ruined buildings until it was safe to make a dash across the empty roadway. On the west side they smelled horses long before they found them behind the parish church.

The animals stopped their thirsty pacing at sight of three shadows flattening against the rear of the church. They pushed in together along the east side of the corral to stand motionless, eyes ahead, watching.

Jose Duarte cocked his head, straining to hear riders coming. All he heard was hooves fidgeting in deep corral dust. He touched Moraga's arm. 'We can open the gate and start them north. The others can pick them up north of here. Batista, they are going to find that dead man. They will know there are enemies out here in the night.'

Garcia growled. 'Be quiet, Jose. Free-running horses go in all directions and three men on foot can't make them go in the right direction. Settle down. Wait.'

Batista wiped his lips. He was thirsty. Jerky caused thirst and he'd been chewing pieces of it the way other men lighted quirleys.

Without warning a man cried out in a wild scream over in the direction of the *cantina*. Jose Duarte had been right. Batista had not doubted that the other drinkers in the *cantina* would find the dead *rurale*, he just did not expect it to happen so soon.

Duarte slipped back to look down the south side of the church. Men came out of the *cantina* waving guns and yelling at one another. Jose scuttled back to tug at the *mayordomo*'s sleeve. 'It will be only a few minutes when they will come over here. Batista, inside the church!'

Duarte did not wait. He ran into the church with Pifas Garcia behind him. The last man to enter was Batista. He had been listening very hard for the sound of riders coming down the east side of the village.

CHAPTER EIGHT

A LONG NIGHT

The church's walls were three feet thick. Starlight came from the building's only window in the front wall, which had been smashed, and the wide doorway from which the panels had been torn away.

The hiding men had no idea how old the church was and at this time did not care, but it was very old. It had the ingrained incense-scent of very old churches.

The altar was to their right, eerily limned by very weak, reflected starlight. There was a large crucifix above and behind the altar. Like most Mexican wall adornments of this kind, there was an ornate background of gold-plated fire behind the dark Cross.

There were also bulletholes but in darkness they were invisible.

Batista inched close to the rear opening and peeked out. So far none of the raging men from the *cantina* had come over to the corral, but their yells, hair-curling oaths, rang through the abandoned town. Someone even fired off a few rounds from his handgun, and while the men in the dark church listened, the shooting did not cause them particular anxiety; agitated armed Mexicans fired weapons at everything and nothing.

Batista prayed for the arrival of John Burket and his horsemen. They could have been out back and the men inside the church would have been unable to hear them.

Briefly, startlingly, a man with outflung arms appeared in the church doorway, barely recognisable by the hiding watchers who aimed weapons at him. But the man twisted away with a fierce oath and was lost to sight from inside the old mud building.

Pifas leaned to address Batista. 'The sergeant.'

Moraga nodded and breathed another fervent prayer. Eventually, when the drunken soldiers and red-flaggers went out to the corral, it was a certainty that some of them would rush forward to search the church.

If Burket's men survived, they would be dragged to the roadway and forced to run for their lives. Batista had a sudden, very clear image of Señora Alvarado y O'Bryan. It came and went in seconds. If Burket's riders did not appear soon, the señora would have more than her dead husband to mourn over.

There was no sound of riders but there was a very abrupt rattle of gunfire north and perhaps a short distance east of the church. Wildly agitated Mexicans fired back from north and south of the church. This defiance brought back a deafening and continuing roll of gunfire from the northeast. As it increased the forted-up men inside the church could tell that those distant gunmen were coming southward.

Batista shot a swift look in the direction of the shadowed altar, muttered to himself, then watched Pifas Garcia going stealthily towards the rear doorway, and called to him.

Garcia did not hear. The firing was getting closer to the rear of the church. Batista moved swiftly, caught Pifas by the shoulder and hurled him away from the doorway. This time when he spoke the words were audible above the gunfire. 'If you shoot from in here they will force their way inside. You idiot!'

Garcia was rigidly motionless for several seconds, then wheeled to go back among the pews where Duarte and Ramon Cruz were crouching.

Burket's men were pressing the fight. Because they outnumbered the Mexicans it was inevitable that the defenders would be forced back. There was some shouting, mostly indistinguishable, all of it in Spanish as the *rurales* and their companions gave ground.

Eventually they did not fire from around the church. There was a long lull in the noise. Batista rose from the floor and sank down upon a wooden pew, sixgun dangling.

Abruptly the gunfire started again, but this time out in the roadway and with fewer guns being fired. Pifas got up, sank down beside Moraga, looked at the older man and wagged his head. He glanced over his shoulder, twisted violently from the waist and fired the second his handgun had cleared the back of the bench.

There was another gunshot. Both

explosions sounded almost at the same time. Plaster fell from the ceiling, and struck Batista, driving him back to the floor.

Pifas fired again. Outside, guns firing from the upper end of town increased in number while the guns of the Mexicans fired less and with longer periods of quiet between shots.

Pifas leaned to help Batista to his feet. He grinned at the *mayordomo* and pointed with his pistol in the direction of the roadway doors. There was a man lying flat out on his face half inside, half outside the church.

The roadway racket ended but the smell of burned gunpowder was strong and would remain so for many days.

Batista walked to the wide doorless front opening and stood looking at the man Pifas Garcia had shot. It was Sergeant Escobar. Batista shook his head and stepped past the body to one side of the doorway to gaze into the eerily starlighted empty roadway.

Men were sidling southwards toward the centre of town, appearing briefly, fading from sight and re-appearing elsewhere. He recognised several of them. One was John Burket, another was that bear-built teamster who had climbed down from the wagon to hurl down his hat and swear.

Jose came up, leaned to look and pulled back as he said, '*Jefe*, one Mexican looks like another Mexican in the night.'

That was true. Batista returned to the

benches and sat down, raised his eyes to the pale figure behind the altar and felt the tiredness leave his entire body. He smiled, made a little Sign in the darkness and watched Duarte and Ramon Cruz go toward the rear doorway. Someone was out there at the corral.

Pifas also went back there. He called to the men out back, identified himself by name, told them who was with him inside the church, and moved clear of the doorway as several men walked over and stepped inside. One of them removed his hat, the others didn't.

The man who had removed his hat was the border-breed Esteven McCoy. Batista went back to meet them. One of the stockmen ran a filthy sleeve over his face before speaking. 'There's a couple of 'em in the saloon. The rest are dead. Where the hell did all them horses come from?'

Batista told them what he and the others had decided about that and the rancher seemed to accept it. He was about to speak again when gunfire erupted across the wide roadway in the area of the *cantina*. All the men in the church went up to the front doorless opening where they could see the saloon. They could also see several of Burket's men over there. One of them called out in Spanish. His answer came back from inside the saloon in the same language. It was a refusal to accept the earlier demand for surrender. The speaker lent emphasis to his refusal by firing blindly from one side of the saloon doorway.

That was a mistake. There were men in position on both sides of the old church for exactly this purpose. They could slant bullets inwards on each side of the doorway from across the road.

Another lull followed their fierce firing. Not until the last echo was gone did the same man who had called out before, do so again. This time he got no answer.

The silence ran on. Esteven leaned from behind Ramon Cruz and said, 'They are dead.'

Pifas Garcia called to Burket's men in English, telling them to hold their fire. He would see if anyone remained alive in the saloon.

Batista raised a restraining hand but Pifas was already moving ahead out of reach.

There was no sound as Garcia strode into the roadway, but several men moved away from shelter to watch. Pifas reached the centre of the road, looked left and right and continued forward.

The *cantina*'s front wall did not have a square foot of exposed surface that had not been badly scarred by bullets. The door was still hanging on its hinges but the wood had been shredded.

Pifas reached the front of the building, stepped clear of the doorway, hitched at his shellbelt and leaned to speak softly in Spanish. 'If you are alive in there, tell me so.'

The silence continued, there was no answer. Two men with carbines eased around the north side of the building. One was Charley Dawes. He called to Garcia. 'Leave 'em be, friend.' He held out a hand with a little dented bucket in it. 'Move back. Come back where we are an' I'll toss this thing through the doorway.' Dawes grinned. 'There's enough black powder in here to lift that little building plumb off the ground. See this black thing? That there's the fuse. Now move up towards us so's I'll have some room.'

Pifas sidled northward along the *cantina*'s wall towards Dawes and his friend, then halted because although anyone listening to what Dawes had said from as far away as the church could have heard what had been said, Dawes had spoken in English. South of the border not everyone understood English. The farther one got from the border the less likely it was that people would understand it.

He shuffled back closer to the doorway and repeated what Dawes had said in Spanish. There was more silence. Charley Dawes was getting impatient. He said, 'Come on back here, damn it. We're wastin' time. Dawn'll be here directly and we still got a long way to go.'

Pifas heard a soft sound from inside, like a groan. He was the only one close enough to hear it. 'There's a live one in there,' he told Dawes over his shoulder, and got back a curt reply.

'All right. Get away from the door an' I'll put him out of his misery.'

Pifas leaned closer. This time the sound was more clearly audible. It sounded more like a kitten than a human being. He raised an arm backwards to keep Charley Dawes from approaching, stepped to the ruined door, gave it a hard punch and it fell inside the dark room.

Across the road Batista held his breath. This was the moment for whoever was in there to fire his gun.

There was no gunshot. Pifas used his pistol-barrel to push aside the scrap of door-frame still being held upright by hinges, cocked his weapon and stepped fully inside.

There was a dead soldier on one side of the door and a dead *rurale* on the opposite side of it. He recognised the *rurale* as that friendly man who had smiled a lot after the fight north of the border.

Back where faint light reached the bar something pale was trying to drag itself away. Pifas crossed the room in five wide steps and pointed his gun into the upturned, white face of a woman.

They looked at one another for five seconds before Pifas moved the pointed gun away and asked in Spanish who was behind the bar. She answered in the same language that there was no one back there; that there had been no one in the saloon except the dead men near the doorway.

He sank to one knee. She had been hit by two bullets, one through the calf of her leg, which had not broken the bone, the other, which made a bloody wound and looked to be the worse of the two but which actually had done no more than gouge the flesh of her upper left arm, had been a deep graze.

She was holding her lower lip between her teeth. She was perhaps in her late twenties with a round face smudged with dirt, and black eyes that looked back at Garcia with a dull expression of resignation.

He yelled for Batista and tore cloth from her skirt to bind the bloody arm. Charley Dawes entered, still holding the home-made bomb. He was examining the dead men near the door when Batista, Jose Duarte and Ramon Cruz rushed in.

Other men arrived, holding guns and stepping warily. John Burket came over to the bar to watch Batista working on the woman. He leaned and asked in English if she would die. In that poor light she seemed to be covered with blood.

Batista's reply was curt. 'No. You had

better go get those horses heading north and start your wagon back too. On a still night all that noise carries for miles. The soldiers will have heard it unless they are fifty miles away.'

Burket straightened up, spoke to the men and led the way out of the *cantina*. Cruz and Duarte went with them. At the doorway they met Esteven McCoy, told him curtly about the injured woman and took him with them back across the road.

Batista fashioned splints for the woman's leg from broken chairs. He sent Pifas behind the bar for tequila. He helped the woman sit erect with her leg straight in front, and smiled at her as he wiped blood on his trousers. 'You will be all right. We will take care of you. Do you live in Dolores?'

She answered in Spanish and Batista took the bottle from Pifas and held it for her to swallow twice before handing it back. The woman gasped and grimaced. Batista asked about her family.

She had no family. They had all perished during a fever that had passed through the village four years earlier. The men exchanged a look and Batista shrugged as he pushed up off his knees. 'The soldiers will be here after daybreak. They will have a doctor with them.'

Pifas looked at the woman and said, 'No. We won't leave her for the soldiers.'

'She can't ride with that injured leg, Pifas.'

'Then she will ride in the wagon, Batista.'

The *mayordomo* looked down. She was a pretty woman, even covered with dirt and blood, and she was still biting her lip to keep from crying out. He leaned and brushed hair from her face. 'She is brave,' he said in English. 'All right. Find some blankets, anything we can make a sling out of and we will carry her. And hurry, Pifas. No matter how many miles we cover they will probably overtake us before we reach the border.'

Outside there was the sound of shouting men and running horses, a great many horses. When Batista and Pifas got the woman between them on an old brown blanket, and reached the centre of the road, there was a pair of mounted men trailing two saddled horses. One of the men was Charley Dawes. His jaws were working rhythmically and calmly. He looked down, turned aside to expectorate, then dismounted, handed Batista his reins, took the woman in his arms like a child and jerked his head for the others to head for the wagon on horseback.

He carried the woman as though she were weightless, and continued to chew his cud as though carrying women wounded by gunfire was something he did every day.

CHAPTER NINE

TOWARDS DAWN

Four riders went with the horses, the others remained with the wagon. The teamster could not make good time until they got clear of the barren low hills on the east side of Dolores. Once he was on flat ground he whistled up his hitch.

But the wagon slowed the riders. Dawes sent two men back to listen for pursuit. No one really expected there to be any but Charley Dawes had been a soldier. In times like these he thought as one.

When they had put the woman over the tailgate of the wagon and she had seen that big gun above her nearly filling the rig, her eyes were as round as spur rowels. Batista pointed out to her that regardless of how the wagon tilted and wobbled, the gun would not roll back on her because its wheels had been blocked in front and behind.

He rode with her for a while, trailing his reins over the tailgate. She was in pain and Batista had not thought to bring a bottle from the *cantina*.

He made her as comfortable as he could, using bedrolls and small bags of coffee, sugar and flour. The only time the wagon really bucked and wobbled was when it was being driven fast, which was not very often. The teamster was experienced; regardless of how much he would have liked to have made a run for it, he knew exactly how to get the most out of his team without having them fail in harness. The gun was large and it was heavy. Additional weight had been added by men pitching their bedrolls and sacks of supplies into the rig.

Batista climbed over the tailgate, stepped into a stirrup and rode in search of his friends from the ranch. As soon as he approached them Pifas Garcia turned back towards the rear of the wagon. Jose Duarte grinned slyly at Batista about this but said nothing.

There was a little sporadic conversation. Otherwise the horsemen paced their mounts to the speed of the wagon.

Burket came back to ride a while with Batista. They discussed what had happened. Burket already knew about the *rurale* whose throat had been cut, but he did not know why, so Batista told him of the murdered priest.

It turned chilly. To the riders cold came before dawn. It was still too dark for visibility to be very good, but without a doubt this condition was going to change shortly.

Charley Dawes rode in the drag in order to be the first to hear from the riders he had a mile or so to the rear. Charley's error was an understandable one; it had been made dozens of times under similar circumstances. He was concentrating on pursuit, which would come from the south, and did not think of the possibility of danger being up ahead northward. Neither did anyone else until Dolores was about five miles behind, the pre-dawn chill made men button jackets to the throat, and a very thin and irregular slit of dull grey began to firm up along the distant horizon.

The night was hushed except for sounds of moving horses. The notes of a bugle sounded muted by distance but unmistakable as John Burket started up towards the front of the column where the wagon was.

Charley pulled straight up in his saddle, jaws slack for a moment or two, then he spurred towards the front where John Burket was riding. The teamster was sitting perfectly erect looking above the ears of his horses into the northward night. He had been as surprised as everyone else had been.

He turned as Dawes came up and said, 'How in the hell did they get around us and up that close to the line?'

Charley had no answer. No one had one. Charley leaned to say he would ride ahead, but John Burket held up a hand. 'Not alone. Take someone with you.'

'Who?'

'Batista Moraga.'

Dawes spun rearward and rode down the column until he saw the *mayordomo*, then he called and beckoned, whirled back and did not even glance over his shoulder to see whether Batista was following him.

He was. The bugle had startled him as it had everyone else. As he loped ahead in the wake of his companion, he tried to imagine how those lancers had got around, and up that far. It was difficult to believe they had done that. If they had been close enough to the village to hear gunfire they would not have ridden around it to get up north. They would have aimed directly for Dolores.

Dawes slackened to a walk until Batista was beside him, then wagged his head. 'They had to have wings,' he growled.

Batista said nothing for a while as they slouched along. 'They could have done it,' he finally said to the former Confederate. 'But why? The fight was back at the village. Maybe they knew who we were, otherwise what sense does it make for them to try and cut us off before we reach the border?'

Dawes was groping for his plug and rode in silence until he had pouched a cud into his cheek, then he smiled through the feeble light, spat, and said, 'They sure as hell got scouts out.' He gestured ahead through the paling-out night-gloom. 'Makes a man feel like a crow on a fence, don't it? Real handy targets, *mayordomo*.'

Batista twisted to glance rearward. The sound of the wagon was clearly audible but the riders were either making no noise or they were too far back to be heard. He straightened forward and rubbed his stubbly chin. The thirst, which he had completely forgotten, returned now, otherwise he might have rummaged for a twist of jerky.

Dawes raised a hand. They halted to listen, but except for the rattling wagon with its steel tyres grating over stone-hard *caliche* there was nothing to be heard. But as they were leaning to start their mounts moving again, Dawes sat back peering straight ahead. His jaws were not moving. Batista who had decided a couple of days ago that he could not hear as well as he once had been able to, waited until the lanky man spoke quietly without turning his head. 'They're comin' due south down this damned road.' He spared a moment to gaze quizzically at Batista because he was more puzzled than ever. The lancers would know they were trying to reach the border by the roadway.

Batista, whose hearing in fact really had been subtly becoming less acute for the past year or so without him being aware of it, had no trouble at all hearing someone up ahead through the darkness laugh loudly a moment before someone snarled in Spanish.

Dawes was sitting like a statue, scowling and chewing. Batista interpreted for him. 'He said he was sick and tired of having to leave his blankets in the middle of the night and ride on an empty stomach.'

Comprehension hit Batista Moraga like a mule kick. He whirled his horse and called to Charley Dawes. 'The gun. Hurry with me.'

Dawes asked no question as he too headed back for the wagon and its escort in a quick lope. They came upon John Burket riding slightly ahead. When Burket halted to await them everyone else also halted, including the teamster and his wagon.

Batista said, '*Jefe*, it is not the lancers. It is an army of *pronunciados*. Maybe the same army the soldiers chased away from Dolores a few days ago.' Burket glanced swiftly at Dawes, who sat and chewed and shrugged wide shoulders, spat, and said, 'Damned if I know. Only it never seemed to me it could be them lancers.'

Burket raised his head to listen. The sound was out there, very faint but clearly audible; mounted men, wagons, and a large party of men walking on foot. He raised an arm to signal the teamster to lead off going eastward away from the roadway. Batista interrupted. 'It won't do any good. Did you ever see a Mexican rebel army? It has no order. There will be soldiers and their *soldaderas* a mile on both sides of the road. The main body will

97

be on the road, but if it is a large army it may even be scattered two or three miles to the east and west.'

Burket dropped his arm and scowled ahead where the sounds were louder now. Also, visibility was improving. Not enough for either force to see the other yet, but soon it would happen.

Pifas Garcia rode up as did other horsemen. They could also hear the noise. Batista eased up in the saddle as he said, 'At least it is too early in the day for them to be drinking. *Jefe*, we can't escape them.' He jutted his head in the direction of the wagon. 'Turn it so that the tailgate is facing northward up the road. Wait until their scouts see us, then tie back the canvas so they can see the gun. I will ride up and tell them our leader wants to palaver with their leader.

'If it works, they will let us pass. If it don't work, you can use the gun and kill a hundred of them before they can get away. They know that. They know what Gatling guns are.'

Charley Dawes's eyes were twinkling sardonically as he listened to the elderly *mayordomo*. John Burket sat so long in silence Batista had almost despaired when Burket said, 'You and Garcia go ahead until you can see them.' Burket leaned to hold forth a large white handkerchief. 'Flag them with it, Batista. Tell their commander what we want—passage to the border, no one to follow, no one to snipe or bushwhack, or we will start firing the gun.'

Charley Dawes swung to the ground as he watched Pifas Garcia and Batista Moraga ride northward at a liver-bruising trot. He said, 'I think that's the first time I ever seen Messicans trot horses.' He glanced up but if John Burket had heard him he gave no indication of it.

He turned back, leaned to speak curtly to the teamster, then straightened in the saddle to tell the others what was to be done.

Travis Moore, the diminutive Texan, looked doubtful. 'How many of 'em?' he asked, and when no one could answer he said, 'Hell, if it's a fightin' band of *pronunciados* there'll be hundreds of 'em, and we don't have nowhere near that much ammunition for the gun.'

No one argued with him. What was obvious was that less than thirty men, even with a Gatling gun, could not last long against an entire army of rebels if it came to a battle. This was one of those times when letting someone know you had such a murderous weapon might be better than firing the damned thing.

They waited. The sound of marching men was clearly audible as the teamster turned his wagon, got it back on the roadbed and crawled back through to pull loose the pucker-string that held the canvas closed above the tailgate. He did not even glance at the wounded woman but she watched everything he did. When he lifted a long, straight magazine from a box and rammed it into the slot to load the big, grey gun, her eyes got perfectly round. He yanked back on a lever, tipped the weapon until its multiple muzzles were aimed straight up the middle of the road, then he leaned, looked at the silent horseman, and made a death's-head smile.

He was ready.

Charley Dawes led his horse to the front of the wagon and left it tied there as he walked back towards the tailgate trailing his carbine and rhythmically chewing. The others followed his example.

They squatted on both sides of the wagon to wait. The Texas gunfighter chewed on a stick of jerky. Everyone squinted through the brightening, cold dawn. Dawes made a humorous remark and they laughed a little.

It was a long wait, because after Pifas and Batista encountered the advance of the insurgent army they were not escorted back where the rebel officers were until they had had their weapons taken from them, along with everything they had in their pockets.

The insurgent chieftain was an ugly, very dark man, short and thick with coarse black hair. He had jet-black small eyes that seemed never to blink. He wore a split-hide charro jacket and tight trousers both of which were elaborately embroidered. Neither he nor his clothes looked to Batista Moraga as though they had been anywhere near soap and water for several months.

He was chewing on a long, thin Mexican cigar when Moraga and Garcia were brought up to him. He stopped chewing and stared at them. The escorting *bandolero* started to explain but the barrel-built dark man waved him into silence and walked completely around the visitors, halted in front where the scent of stale sweat, garlic and horses was in their faces, then he asked curtly who they were and what they were doing here.

Batista told him. Pifas looked coldly at the officer and said nothing. The officer ignored him, listened carefully to Batista, and when Moraga finished speaking the officer smiled around his soggy, unlighted cigar and said, 'So that was it? The horses; we heard them running past in the night. I thought it was soldiers trying to get around us, so we struck camp and started back to Dolores.' Having said this much the Mexican chewed his cigar briefly before speaking again. 'How many with your party?'

Batista replied shortly. 'About twenty-five men.'

'And this gun—where is it, then?'

'In a wagon in the middle of the road about a mile southward.' Batista also smiled. 'Aimed straight up the roadway.'

'And there is ammunition?'

Batista made a little casual gesture and told a big lie. 'Plenty, *jefe*. Enough to kill your army. It can be swivelled from left to right and it fires farther than your rifles.' The smile lingered as Batista gave a little shrug. 'You can probably overrun twenty-five men, *commandante*, but by the time you do it you will not have enough men left to meet the army and the lancers who will be coming up our back-trail.'

The Mexican spat out his cigar, squinted southward, turned to gaze at the small crowd of his men who had edged up to listen, then faced Batista again. 'And you want us to let you go past up across the border?'

'Yes. No coming after us, no ambushing, just move aside so we can go back across the border.'

The officer bobbed his head up and down very quickly, little black eyes glowing with slyness. 'All right. You can go. We will not trouble you. Just ride back up where you came from. But you will leave the gun and its ammunition.'

Pifas Garcia hooked both thumbs in his shellbelt and regarded the insurgent chieftain sourly. 'And get riddled in the back,' he said softly.

The officer turned on him. 'You could get shot right here.'

Batista, recognising the quick tendency to violence in them both, broke in to say, 'It's not my gun. Before I can agree to leave it to you we'll have to go back and talk to our leader.'

The officer spat, thought a moment then gave an order to the men behind him to bring his horse, and to mount up to ride with him. He would go talk to the man who owned the Gatling gun. Meanwhile, he told his subordinates, the men could rest, care for their animals and eat breakfast.

CHAPTER TEN

TROUBLE COMES IN BUNCHES

The teamster, who was standing higher than the others, saw riders approaching and called ahead to John Burket.

By the time they could make out Garcia and Moraga the teamster had re-aligned his Gatling gun and was standing back by the crank, a prudent but unnecessary precaution.

There was absolute silence as the insurgents arrived at the wagon where *norteamericanos* bristling with weapons waited.

The Mexican officer dismounted and smiled as he said, 'I am General Eusebio Martinez.' He did not look at Burket, Dawes, not even the men like Ramon Cruz, Jose Duarte and Esteven McCoy who were with the *gringos*. He looked steadily at the menacing Gatling gun inside the wagon. He seemed fascinated by the weapon. Still staring at the gun he told John Burket what he had said to Pifas and Batista where they had met up the road. Everyone could pass without being molested in exchange for the gun. They could even take it out of the wagon. Place it on the ground on its wheels, and keep their wagon.

John Burket considered the short, thick man and his stained, unshaven *bandolero* escort. A number of ranchers had pooled funds to buy the Gatling gun. They were very expensive. They were also rare and hard to come by, and quite obviously the *commandante*'s fascination was prompted by the knowledge that if he had such a weapon no federal route army with cannon mounted on sleds and possibly ten times as many men as he had would be able to stop him, or defeat him.

General Martinez turned from the gun to scowl at Burket. He spoke in Spanish with an unfamiliar guttural accent. 'Unload the gun and you can pass,' he said.

Burket's answer was also in Spanish, border-Spanish which was thoroughly ungrammatical but understandable. 'I think, Commander, that we will go with the gun in the wagon to the border. Then, if you want to pay for it, you can have the gun.'

General Martinez's very dark features froze. 'I will pay for it; I will let you and your men cross the border. I am giving you your life. That is a very high price, is it not?'

Burket gravely inclined his head. 'A very high price, Commander. But not until we reach the border.'

General Martinez bared his teeth. Two of Burket's men tipped up their carbines a little at the other Mexicans. Charley Dawes, listening and chewing, spoke in a soft drawl. 'General, we shot up the village last night. Killed some soldiers and *rurales*. There were lancers coming up from the south. By now they will have reached Dolores. They will not be very far behind us. Behind them is their route army. The longer we stand here the closer they will be getting.'

Martinez snarled. 'Unload the gun!'

Burket raised his gaze to the escort of *bandoleros*. 'If you dismount, you will never mount again. Not in this world.'

The insurgents squirmed but did not dismount.

Burket addressed the officer again. 'It is no more than a mile and a half to the border,

General. You can come with us if you wish. When we cross the line you can have the gun.'

General Martinez was in a rage. Without speaking he turned to mount his horse. Batista Moraga intercepted him, took the reins and shook his head. 'No, Commander. You will ride in the wagon.'

Batista was holding the reins in his right hand when Martinez moved swiftly to draw his sixgun. Behind him a sharp voice called out. 'Draw it and I'll kill you.'

The diminutive Texan, Travis Moore, had already drawn. When Martinez turned just his head, Moore cocked his weapon. Three seconds passed before General Martinez moved his hand away from the hip-holster, looked at his escort and snarled an order to them. 'Go back. Clear the road. No one is to even touch a weapon. After the *gringos* have passed you will follow with more men until we reach the border. Everyone else is to prepare for battle. Go!'

The escort raised a high dust in their haste to go back to the main column of insurgents. General Martinez stamped past to the front of the wagon, climbed up and stopped when the teamster said, 'Shuck that pistol, mister.' Someone had to interpret before Martinez understood and turned indignantly toward John Burket. Burket simply nodded his head. Martinez lifted out his gun, dropped it and

106

when the teamster gestured for him to move past the gun to the front seat, Martinez saw the injured woman, faltered a moment, then moved past.

They got the wagon turned northward again with horsemen on each side of it. Charley Dawes hung back looking for the two men he had sent down the back-trail. There was no sign of them, which could have been good; if they had seen oncoming lancers they would be visible riding hell for leather. Unless of course they had been caught by Mexican soldiers.

He looped his reins to slice off a fresh chew. Up ahead dust was rising. The sun had arisen without Charley being aware of it. It was still chilly but at least visibility was good.

Three quarters of a mile ahead there was a great straggle of curious humanity lining the roadway. Armed men stood like stones as the wagon approached. Not a word was said. Charley thought it might be a good idea to lope up closer to the others when he heard a distant, faint shout and halted to look back.

His scouts were coming in a dead run. Charley stood in his stirrups to see beyond them. There was rising dust a mile farther southward but he could not see what was making it.

When the riders came up and hauled down to a sliding halt one of them yelled at

Charley, 'Lancers. One hell of a lot of them.'

'That's all, just lancers?' Dawes asked, and got a look of incredulity from the scouts.

'Is that all? You danged fool, there's a double line of them stretching back farther than a man can see.'

Charley led off in a lope to catch up with the wagon. He rode past it until he found John Burket riding with a pair of grizzled, greying, fierce-looking cowmen. Charley gestured. 'Mex lancers comin' up fast. Maybe a whole regiment of 'em.'

Batista rolled his eyes and looked pityingly at Pifas Garcia. 'We are between. We are in the middle with insurgents up ahead and on both sides of us, and a regiment of lancers coming up behind us. If one don't kill us the others will.'

Burket shouted at the teamster, who whistled up his hitch. The little band rode past staring Mexicans for more than half a mile before the harness-horses had to be hauled down to a walk. General Martinez leaned out to look back. The teamster, who was a large, burly man with a thick sorrel beard, caught him by the shoulder and yanked him back. 'Set still,' he exclaimed, saw the blank look he was getting, and swore loudly until Ramon Cruz came up. He then jabbed at the Mexican general with a thumb and said, 'Tell that darned mud-coloured *bandolero* to set still on the seat, not to lean

108

out to look back and not to try to jump out or I'll cut his blessed gullet from side to side. Tell him that!'

Cruz did not interpret properly. He simply said that if General Martinez tried to jump from the wagon the teamster would kill him. Then Cruz dashed ahead to find Jose Duarte with whom he had been riding stirrup.

Martinez made his menacing broad smile at the teamster, who reached inside his shirt, drew out a wicked-bladed big knife and held it in his hand. Martinez stopped smiling and moving.

A rattle of gunfire broke out farther back. It inspired the teamster to urge his horses into another gallop, but they could not maintain it so he let them drop down to a trot, a gait they could keep up for a long while.

There was more gunfire farther back. There was also dust. It was on both sides of the road, out a fair distance. Batista thought the rebels had engaged the lancers but it was impossible to make out much in the dust.

The firing diminished to pot-shooting with intervals between. The teamster brought his hitch down to a steady walk and growled when his agitated passenger wanted to lean out again. General Martinez protested loudly in Spanish, gesturing with both hands. The big man with the sorrel beard ignored him.

John Burket turned back from the lead,

rode aside a short distance and sat out there looking southward. When the wagon came up he rode over beside it and told the teamster to halt where he was. The teamster looked startled, then, as he eased back on the lines to stop the wagon, he yelled to Burket. 'How close are they?'

Burket was already riding away. Pifas Garcia came up on the off-side and exchanged hostile glares with the Mexican general, and told the teamster that the lancers were going around the foot-soldiers. He thought they were coming after the wagon and its *gringo* escort.

The teamster yelled at his horses until he had them aligned, then set the binders, ignored General Martinez and clambered back towards the tailgate. His Gatling gun still had the tall magazine rising above the rear of the gun. He almost fell over the wounded woman as he reached to yank the tailgate-canvas aside.

Pifas had been correct. The reason the heavy firing had stopped was that the lancers were coming up the east side of the road out of carbine range, in pursuit of the *gringos* and their wagon.

John Burket with several companions returned to the wagon where the sweating teamster was swivelling his gun. Others also came back, some to dismount and hold the harness-horses.

Everyone was watching the lancers. They were uniformed, which was only common in a Mexican route-army among those who rode horses. They had long wooden lances, tipped with brass. From each lance held by a horseman upon which his line was to dress itself evenly fluttered a small pennant.

When Batista could see the little pennants he yelled at the teamster. The noise was continuous and deafening. The harness-horses responded as much to the abrupt vibrations of the wagon as they did to the continuous gunfire coming from the rear of the wagon.

Dust rose in clouds as Mexican soldiers fought their mounts around to flee. The teamster continued to crank his rotating gunbarrels and swing his gun. Outside the wagon men cheered at the tops of their voices. A few even fired after the routed lancers, but they did not have weapons with that kind of range.

Batista felt a tug at his arm and turned. General Martinez was standing there, mouth open, breathing hard and laughing.

Farther back, insurgents had used the time after their little skirmish with the lancers had ended, to saddle up. They broke away from the road in shouting pursuit, shooting indiscriminately as they rode hard to overtake the *federales*. Again the dust became too thick to see what was happening, but no one cared. What mattered was that their Gatling gun had won them enough time to reach the border and cross it.

Burket yelled sharp orders. As the invaders started north again only one individual remained back where they had been: General Eusebio Martinez. He was waving with both hands and yelling for someone to bring him a horse.

They were within sight of one of the little whitewashed cairns of round stones which marked the boundary between Mexico and the United States, when Batista rode up on the wagon's near-side, stepped from his saddle to the floorboards and while holding his reins at arms' length, jostled the sweating teamster.

'You didn't hit any of them,' he exclaimed.

The teamster glared. 'I didn't try to hit any of them. That ain't fighting, that's like shootin' pigeons perchin' on a tree limb. I didn't want to kill no one, I just wanted to let 'em know what we had in the wagon. Make 'em turn back an' leave us alone. Are you bloodthirsty? I ain't.'

Batista stepped back across saddle-leather laughing. Charley Dawes, who had gone back a short distance to see what he could, came loping up grinning widely. He pulled down to a trot between Batista Moraga and Travis Moore. 'Damnedest sight. The fat

112

beaner's troops are chasin' them fancy lancers on horseback an' on foot, raisin' so much dust can't neither bunch see much of the others. Boys, it's a rout pure an' simple. Does m'heart good to see our side rout someone for a change.'

Dawes loped ahead leaving Travis Moore and Batista Moraga looking after him. Batista said, 'Our side?'

Moore made a crooked smile. 'Yeah. In the war the Yankee cavalry had the most men, the best horses, and more damned guns'n a man could shake a stick at. They chased the Secesh cavalry ten ways from the middle. You understand?'

Batista nodded looked back where the gunfire was brisking up again although it was not possible to make out the battle, if one was in progress back there, because of the dust.

He straightened forward as the teamster stood upright behind his dashboard, tooled his horses past a cairn of white-painted rocks, let go with a howl that could be heard in all directions, then he sat down and put slack in his lines so that the horses could pick their own gait and take their time. They were no longer in Mexico.

Burket kept the men moving until they were several miles northward, then sought shade and halted to dismount and strip his horse. The fight was still audible southward but much less audible than it had been an hour earlier.

They found a little seepage spring to water the stock, then sat down in willow-shade to chew jerky, tank up from canteens, roll smokes or whittle off chews and look at one another. Charley Dawes tilted his head and roared with laughter. Others joined him. Batista looked around. Ramon and Jose were nearby but there was no sign of Pifas Garcia.

He sprang to his feet but was restrained by the powerful arm of Jose Duarte who grinned and shook his head. 'You see there; that is his horse.'

Batista recognised the animal. 'All right. Is he hurt?'

The youngest of them answered while Duarte continued to hold Moraga's leg. 'No, *viejo*, he is not hurt. But you might be if you go climbing into the wagon. Are you blind too? Didn't you notice Pifas was never far from the tailgate when there was trouble?'

Batista shook off Duarte's grip and sank down on the ground. 'The woman? He is looking after her wounds?'

Ramon and Jose rolled their eyes. Cruz said, 'Her wounds? Maybe, *viejo*.'

Jose threw out his arms. 'Never mind,' he told the *remudero*. 'This is what happens when men get old. They forget.'

Batista picked up the innuendo and frowned at them. 'The woman—and Pifas

Garcia?'

Cruz said, 'Why not?'

'Why not!' retorted the *mayordomo*. 'Because we almost got killed, that's why not.'

'Truly,' breathed Ramon Cruz in Spanish. 'It is so when men get old.'

CHAPTER ELEVEN

OVER THE BORDER

The sun was high, heat was increasing and although the little seepage spring was better than no spring at all, its recovery-rate was too slow, so John Burket got his party moving again. They needed more than water, but they certainly needed that. The nearest good source of water was back up at that old roofless *jacal* with the cottonwood trees where they had halted on their way to Mexico. Goat Spring.

For a long while the conversation was about their miraculous escape and no one thought much about the back-trail until the teamster, who had been leaning to look back from time to time, raised a yell and pointed.

Dust, a fair amount of it, and it was rising in the wake of what had to be a fairly large party of horsemen. Charley Dawes spat and wagged his head. He was the first of them to guess what was happening.

'Gen'al Martinez sure as hell. After the gun.'

They halted under a blazing sun to wait and watch. When it was clear that what Charley had surmised was correct, the men dismounted, made their animals fast, took weapons and went to the rear of the wagon.

The teamster, sweating like a stud-horse, had pulled back his tail-gate canvas and was aligning his multi-barrelled gun. Batista Moraga went back there and saw Pifas Garcia already inside the wagon. Batista leaned to look inside where sunshine did not reach. The woman had fresh, clean bandages on her wounds. She smiled wanly at Batista. He turned his back to watch the oncoming riders.

It was the insurgent horsemen, bandoliers with shiny brass cartridges in them, worn across their chests, riding with carbines in one hand, reins in the other hand, bronzed, soiled, dark men maintaining no order as they rode but careful not to get ahead of the stocky man up front, who was astride a handsome sorrel with a flaxen mane and tail. General Martinez.

Pifas came over the tailgate to stand with Batista as he said, 'Maybe seventy-five of them.'

Moraga said nothing.

116

The teamster was cursing because the mob of horsemen did not ride as the lancers had done, in disciplined order. If he used his gun he would have to swivel it from side to side, not aim just spray lead. Targets like those insurgents were difficult to bring down. In some places there was as much as a hundred and fifty yards between riders.

John Burket came around the far side of the wagon with his carbine and two greying, iron-faced cowmen. They too halted to watch the wild, blood-chilling sight of all those careering horsemen.

One of the cattlemen leaned to say something to Burket, who shook his head and spoke loudly. 'They're not in range yet. And I don't like the idea.'

'They're over the line,' exclaimed the stockman.

Burket leaned aside his carbine, lifted his hat to mop off sweat, re-set the hat and looked squarely at the cowman. 'Two hours back you said to let 'em have the gun.'

'Down in Messico,' stated the rancher. 'Down there we had to make a trade to stay alive.'

Travis Moore, who was listening, waved his arm southward. 'You think them little mounds of white stones mean anythin' to them fellers? Not on your tintype they don't. Mister Burket, I heard you tell that Mex general he could have the gun after we was safe across the border. You better keep your word. That's a hell of a lot of armed men out there.'

The Mexican officers were shouting and gesturing for their men to slack off. The entire party was less than a half-mile away before the officers got them lined up on the roadway. Now, they rode at a steady walk, General Martinez out front and directly behind him a glowering Mexican with a badly pock-marked face, who was carrying one of those lances with the little pennant on it.

Charley Dawes grinned. 'Look downright military, don't they?'

No one answered but the old cowman, whose dislike of Mexicans was clear and abiding, spat, hitched at his shellbelt and squinted until his eyes were nearly closed. John Burket addressed him. 'Even if I hadn't said they could have the gun when we were safe, count them. They outnumber us by about ten to one. You tell 'em they can't have the gun and this is as far as any of us will go. Right here full of Mex lead.'

The cowman turned and stamped back up towards the horses where the same men who had held the horses during the early firing were doing it again.

Burket watched him depart and turned back when the other cowman said, 'He's got a right to be mad. He's been losin' livestock to border-jumpers a long time. But as far as I'm concerned they can have the damned gun. Just as long as they take it back down into Messico with them.'

There were murmurs of approval from others who were standing nearby.

General Martinez, no doubt because he could see the ugly snout of the Gatling gun aimed directly down the roadway, raised a hand to halt his men. Then he sat a moment, hands atop the dinnerplate-sized saddlehorn of his *esilla vaquero*, looking steadily ahead.

Batista Moraga went over to John Burket to speak. Before he could do that the General urged his mount ahead at a slow walk. Everyone watched him. There was not a sound until he was within a hundred feet of the wagon's tailgate, where he reined slightly to one side and approached John Burket, expressionless, sweaty and dead calm.

He nodded to Burket, ignored the onlookers and said, 'Now, you are safe. We let you pass. No one even raised a hand against you. We have kept our word. Now—you will keep yours, no?'

The stubborn old cowman was glaring, but he was standing far to one side of the group around Burket. No one else appeared to be as adamant although there were expressions of hostility.

Burket seemed to be having difficulty arriving at a decision. He did not answer for a long while, not until General Martinez loudly sighed, then leaned forward in his saddle and spoke again. 'Look you; this I can tell you about your gun. It cannot be swung left and right as swiftly as horsemen can charge in those directions. You will kill some men but most of them can get around you on both sides where the gun will not help you. We can kill every one of you. Then we will take the gun anyway. You comprehend, friend?'

Burket's eyes did not leave the Mexican. He turned to Travis Moore and several other men and quietly gave an order. 'Let down the tailgate, get plenty of help and lift the gun down into the roadway.'

Martinez scowled, searched among the men around Burket until he saw Batista Moraga, and asked in Spanish what Burket had said. Batista interpreted word for word. General Martinez's entire demeanour changed. He relaxed, he smiled broadly, then he called in Spanish for some of his riders to come forward and help with the gun.

The Gatling was not only very heavy, it was also awkward to lift, but with enough men at work these obstacles were overcome. The moment the big weapon was clear of the wagon, it arose four inches on its springs. Some of Martinez's men had seen the wounded woman. They passed word to

Martinez, who listened, thought briefly then typically shrugged beefy shoulders. 'One woman,' he said in Spanish. 'She is not important. The men with strong horses put lariats on the gun. We will pull it back to our encampment.'

The burly teamster climbed down, pulled three big boxes to the tailgate, muscled them one at a time to the ground and looked up. Martinez, who had been threatened by the teamster, seemed to have forgotten. He grinned, said, 'Thank you,' in Spanish and gestured for the crates to be smashed open and for his horsemen to stuff pockets, saddlebags, even their shirts with bullets.

Finally, as the Mexicans began dragging the wheeled gun southward, General Martinez faced John Burket and saluted. He was smiling.

They remained where they were watching until the insurgents and their newly acquired weapon were close to the invisible line, then struck out in the direction of Hidalgo. Not until they were several miles away did that grim old stockman approach Burket with a comment. 'Them horses we recovered— Lord knows where they are now—don't even come close to what that gun cost, John.'

Burket smiled. 'Yeah, I know. But you an' I are ridin' along right now, which we wouldn't be if we hadn't let them have the gun. How do you figure the value of all our lives? Would you say they are worth what the gun cost?'

The older man slouched along in silence for a while. He turned aside to seek his cronies only when Charley Dawes asked Burket if it might not be a good idea to have some outriders go back southward and keep watch just in case the soldiers or the insurgents decided to come after them.

Burket was agreeable even though he was of the opinion that no one was going to pursue them because they would be too fully occupied in battle very shortly.

They made it all the way back to the roofless *jacal* where the animals had their backs washed, were hobbled to graze for a while, sweaty saddle blankets were turned sun-side up in order to dry before being used again, and the men sank down in cottonwood-shade to eat what was passed out to them. The wagon had been provisioned for a campaign of four or five days. There was plenty of food. Pifas Garcia got a full tin of peaches, took them to the wagon, opened the tin with a knife and watched with a soft smile as the pretty Mexican woman drank peach-syrup and ate the fruit. She was sweaty, perhaps feverish, which Garcia noted but did not comment about. He was terrified of infection. She may have thought about it too but neither of them mentioned it.

Her wounds were badly swollen, the flesh discoloured, but there was no longer any more bleeding except for an occasional drop or two.

Pifas could not make the inside of the wagon cool, but he brought her a canteen, made her pallet comfortable, and hovered like an anxious mother. She smiled at him, black eyes soft with appreciation.

They talked, each telling the other of their lives, of their pasts, and she shyly mentioned her hopes, which were to recover, never to go back below the border, and to make a new life somewhere, anywhere, that was not inhabited by people who every year or two went on rampages of murder and pillage.

When they were ready to ride again Pifas went up ahead with Batista and told the older man about the woman. He also told him he would marry the woman. Batista was by now not surprised at their interest in each other, although he had a little difficulty understanding how an attraction could prosper when armed horsemen were threatening in all directions.

He said, 'Will she marry you?'

Pifas had not mentioned the idea to the woman. He looked at the *mayordomo*. 'Am I ugly?' he asked in Spanish.

Moraga answered in the same language. 'Not ugly. But sometimes foolish.'

Pifas's dark colour got a pink tint, his dark

eyes were fixed on the older man as they slouched along. A hundred or so feet of riding passed before he suddenly grinned. 'Isn't everybody foolish, old one?'

'Yes. Every day someone, everyone I suppose, is foolish. It may be, companion, that this should not be for maybe more than a half-hour of each day. You ... I have known you since childhood. Sometimes, you manage to be foolish an entire day.' Batista grinned back. 'Well, I've seen this change in others when they had something besides themselves to live for. What is her name?'

'Maria Teresa Holquin y Bohorquez.'

'Go then and ask Maria Teresa Holquin y Bohorquez if she will marry you.'

Batista twisted in the saddle to watch Pifas Garcia go back down the straggling line to the rear of the wagon. As he straightened around Jose Duarte and Ramon Cruz came along to travel stirrup with him. Duarte had a question. 'Now do you understand how it is with Epifanio?'

Batista drew himself up in dignity, looked down his hawkish nose and replied shortly, 'I knew how it was before.' Seeing the expression of doubt in the faces of his friends, he also said, 'Is it then, that you think I don't understand what it is that makes people love life?'

Duarte and Cruz exchanged a fast look before the younger man responded. 'Of

124

course you knew, *jefe*. Maybe you have forgotten but you certainly knew once.'

Cruz and Duarte laughed, Moraga reddened and urged his horse away from them.

The heat, which had been oppressive before, now began to weaken as a skirmish-line of soiled and ragged clouds began floating in from the northwest. The perils and tribulations of the last few days were replaced as source of conversation by what was to every desert-dweller without any question the most important event of their lives: Rainfall.

They were discussing the possibility even after they had the town of Hidalgo in sight. It was more important, even, than returning to shade, a bar, a cafe and shack out behind the tonsorial parlour where for ten cents a man could get a chunk of tan lye-soap to bathe with and a frayed towel. After he had lugged bucketful after bucketful of hand-pumped water from the spring-house to the bath-house.

Charley Dawes met his scouts a couple of miles southward. The three men rode in the wake of their companions engrossed in conversation about the gun.

They made no effort to overtake their friends. By the time they reached town and met the four riders who had stampeded those freed horses from the corral behind the *parroquia* in Dolores, Hidalgo's townsmen were thumping backs and buying drinks.

Pifas and Ramon Cruz carried the wounded woman to the cottage of the local *curandera*, who lived, as did other Mexicans, in their own separate but connected village on the east side of town.

Ramon returned to *gringo* town and joined the others in celebrating their safe return, but Pifas remained in the small, poorly lighted *jacal* of the old *curandera* to watch her examine Maria Teresa Holquin's wounds.

The swellings and discoloration had been worrying him since he had first noticed that the wounds looked worse instead of better.

CHAPTER TWELVE

AN EVENTFUL DAY

Tired horses and exhausted men spent what remained of the day in Hidalgo. Before dawn the following morning they drifted apart and left town in small groups heading for their ranches, their homes, and in some cases their families.

Batista was anxious to get back to Alvarado Ranch. He rode eastward in pearly pre-dawn darkness with Ramon Cruz and Jose Duarte.

126

Pifas Garcia had remained behind in Mex town. The riders with Batista Moraga had little to say about this except that the injured woman had not looked likely to recover.

Moraga simply said, 'If there is a God she will recover.'

They had a long ride ahead and were not bringing horses back with them. The animals were corralled at John Burket's ranch. He had told Batista the night before that he would cut out as many animals as *la señora* had lost and drive them to her ranch in a few days.

Morning activity at the ranch caused the approaching riders not to be noticed until they were almost to the yard itself. The scent of cooking fires, the drift of piñon smoke, made Batista fully relax. There had been times, lately, when he had not believed he would ever see this yard again.

At the barn there were riders to greet them, to help care for their animals. One, Gonzalo Gutierrez, still annoyed that the *mayordomo* had not selected him to ride south with the *gringo* stockmen, asked about the horses they had gone to recover.

Batista explained, then spread his hands. 'We couldn't see them very well in the darkness, and afterwards there was too much shooting for us to risk leaving the church. But they will not be of the same quality as the horses we lost.'

127

Jose Duarte offered his opinion of this question. 'We lost maybe fifty head. We will get back maybe fifty head. The quality will not be as good, but fifty horses of poor breeding are better than no horses of good breeding.'

Gutierrez abandoned the discussion. He wanted to know what had happened to Pifas Garcia. Batista was being irritated by the other man's attitude so he turned his back and worked with his horse.

Ramon Cruz explained about the wounded woman and that Pifas had remained behind in Hidalgo to look after her.

Gonzalo Gutierrez stared at Cruz. He clearly was having difficulty associating the rough, quick-tempered *vaquero* he had known so long with a woman. Any woman.

Batista left them to cross toward the *patrón*'s residence. Doña Elena met him in the cool and shaded patio. First, she asked if any of the men had been hurt. Batista replied that they hadn't. Then, suspecting this enquiry from her might be based on the fact that three riders had returned and four had left, he explained about the Mexican woman.

Beautiful Doña Elena's black Irish eyes softened upon the old man, but she did not pursue this topic. She asked about horses. When Batista had explained about that, Doña Elena nodded gently. 'Then it all came right?'

Batista looked towards a shaded old wooden bench. She crossed to it, sat, and motioned for him to join her. She had known the *mayordomo* a long time, and before that her husband had known him much longer and told her many stories about him. She studied his craggy profile, the slightly hawkish nose, the mass of iron-grey hair, the lines and calloused hands.

Once, several years earlier, she had tried to guess his age and had come up with something between sixty-five and seventy-five. Now, in the shade, holding his old hat in both hands between his knees, he looked as resolute as he had always looked, but he also looked tired.

She said, 'What of the Messicans; their army and the army of the insurgents?'

Batista's head came up, his eyes crinkled. '*Señora*, first you must know that the man who drove the wagon was also the man who knew about the gun.'

She nodded.

'Well, I know that he once said he did not like to kill people.' Batista faced her slowly, still faintly amused. 'We gave them the gun and the ammunition for it. They took both and went back down into Mexico to fight the *federales*.'

'And it was bad?' she murmured in Spanish.

Batista's worn, square white teeth showed in a smile. 'No, *Señora*. I will tell you how this was.'

She settled more comfortably on the old bench, rolled her eyes and composed herself. This was going to be one of those times when something would be explained to her by someone who would not be hastened.

'The last of our party to reach Hidalgo was the man Charley Dawes, an old soldier. He and two scouts he had sent southward to listen to the battle, to see it if they could, but I must tell you there is always too much dust when great numbers of men are moving.'

Doña Elena smoothed her skirt, shot a look towards the front door, then met Batista's smile with one of her own. Patience, she knew, was something people developed. They were not born with it. Especially Irish people.

'There was no battle, *Señora*.' Batista waited for the expression of astonishment. Doña Elena politely obliged him.

'No battle?'

'*Si*, no battle. I told you the teamster did not approve of people being killed. He gave them the gun and the ammunition and they hurried back below the border. But when they loaded the magazines for the Gatling gun, and the *federales* saw them doing this, they raced eastward and did not stop for two miles, so said our scouts. And the insurgents

130

did not chase them. Neither did they fire their gun at them.' Batista paused, smile widening. 'You must comprehend, *Señora*, that the teamster who did not like to kill people, and who had given them the gun, had also done something else. While General Martinez and John Burket were having their talk, the teamster pressed soft bullet-lead deep down into the magazines of the Gatling gun. The magazines could be loaded, but the bullets could not go past the lead into the gun to be fired.'

Batista sat there, erect and beaming as though he had just described a miracle.

Doña Elena was a practical woman. 'Couldn't they dig the lead out?'

'Yes, but it would take time. Maybe the rest of the day.'

'And the soldiers; they did not come back after they had not been fired at by the Gatling gun?'

'No, *Señora*. They didn't know the gun could not be fired. What they did know because they could see it was that the rebels had a Gatling gun.' Batista shrugged. 'It would be like whip-breaking a horse; as long as the horse only hears the whip strike the ground he is terrified, but once he is struck by a whip he knows that it does not hurt as much as he was sure it would. You see? The *federales* saw the gun. It was aimed towards them. That it could not be fired was less

131

important right then than the fact that—there it was.'

Batista laughed. He wagged his head. 'A clever *gringo*, that teamster. Wouldn't you say?'

Elena arose from the bench. 'Very clever, but it was a risk, Batista. He might have caused the death of all those insurgents.'

Moraga also arose from the bench. He switched from Spanish to English as he said, 'Risk? There is risk in getting out of bed in the morning. And what you say did not happen.'

Elena could hear voices down at the corrals. She had the incense-fragrance of piñon cooking-fires in her face and otherwise as far as she could see, and much farther, was a land created for men, not women.

She was still learning to understand it and unconsciously she had learned to love it. She brought forth four gold coins and held them out. 'One for each of you. When Epifanio comes home see that he gets his coin.'

Batista looked at the coins then slowly shook his head. 'No, *Señora*.'

'You earned it, each of you. I want to show that I appreciate what you went through for—the ranch. Take it.'

He made no move to take the coins but he raised a kindly expression to her face, and reverted again to Spanish when he spoke. 'There is something better you can do, if you

132

will do it. When Pifas returns, a fiesta. A celebration.'

She slowly returned the coins to a pocket. 'When will he return?'

'*Quién sabe?* Who knows? He is in love with the Mexican woman. When she is able to walk. If she ever is.'

Elena's eyes went quickly to the old man's face and remained there. 'If she ever is?'

'*Señora*, she had bullet holes in her. They look very bad to me. Very swollen, very puffy and purple.'

'Infected wounds, Batista?'

He shrugged and avoided her steady stare. 'I can only tell you they look very bad.'

'Did the doctor in Hidalgo look at her?'

'No, *Señora*, she was taken to a *curandera* in Mex town.'

Elena stood like a statue. She knew about *curanderas*; their poultices of herbs and wet earth, their cures for fever of putting freshly killed chickens, split down the middle, over wounds and binding them there.

She said, 'Saddle a horse for me,' and turned briskly in the direction of the massive old oaken front door with its hand-hammered steel hinges and its extruding bolt-heads to make it impervious to bullets.

Batista stood a long time gazing at the door after she had left him, then with a shrug walked back across the yard towards the barn.

Ramon Cruz was the only person still at the barn. He was tying a hair rope in the ancient, prescribed manner to a large rawhide *jacima*, what the *gringos* called a 'hackamore'. It was as though he had never left the yard; he was doing exactly what he always had done, caring for horse-breaking equipment. When Batista walked in Ramon looked up, expecting to be told the results of the *mayordomo*'s visit to the house. Batista strode past, picked up a rope and passed on through and out back to the corrals.

Ramon put aside his work.

When Moraga returned leading a black horse without a brown hair showing anywhere, Ramon moved without a word to fetch the silver-mounted saddle. The black horse was Doña Elena's favourite mount.

He waited until the *mayordomo* had cuffed the horse until it shone, then approached with the blanket and saddle. As he was putting the blanket in place he looked over the animal's back. 'What is it, Batista?'

'She is going to Hidalgo. I think she is going to have the *gringo* doctor there care for Pifas's Mexican woman.'

Cruz eased the saddle down atop the blanket. 'But he is always drunk.'

Batista did not dispute this. It was common knowledge that the *gringo* medical practitioner drank a lot. But he was still considered a good physician, if not always by

Mexicans usually by *gringos*. Batista said nothing.

By the time they had her horse rigged out, Elena appeared through the heat dressed for riding. They led the horse out of the barn and Batista held the off-stirrup until she had swung across, then he stepped back and said, 'It will be cooler in the evening.'

Her retort had nothing to do with the heat. 'I've had a room at the main-house prepared for her. You can see to it that things are ready when I come back with her.'

'*Señora,* she is badly shot. She cannot ride a horse.'

'There are buggies and wagons for hire in Hidalgo,' Elena retorted, then relented a little because of the look of concern she was getting. She smiled downwards. 'We can look after her better out here. She must have the best possible care.'

Batista nodded and stepped aside as Elena started out of the yard. He muttered to himself that Doña Elena had not even seen the woman, knew nothing about her and would certainly regret acting hastily.

Ramon was leaning in the doorway watching his employer as Batista returned to the shade wagging his head. The younger man faced Moraga with an expression of faint, ironic amusement: Whatever it was, provided it came up abruptly, the *mayordomo*'s instinctive reaction was to oppose it.

He had dragged his feet about going down into Mexico, now he was disgruntled because Doña Elena wanted to help an injured woman. He said, 'Is she going to bring her here?'

'Yes. She has had a room prepared for her over at the *hacienda*.' When Batista finished speaking he raised his eyes to the younger man's face. 'If she dies, then what?'

Ramon was unperturbed. 'You mean the Mexican woman? We will bury her in the ranch cemetery as we have buried others.'

Batista sank down in barn-shade. Ramon turned so that he was facing inwards at the barn-opening. 'Look at the pleasant side,' he said in Spanish. 'If she marries Epifanio and moves into his *jacal* it will be good for him. Maybe for them both. You know, he has needed someone for a long time.'

Batista arose, turned his back and shuffled out back to the corrals. Ramon shrugged and returned to his seat and the tying of the mecate he had been doing earlier.

Women!

Jose Duarte and Gonzalo Gutierrez were out there with a quivering, glassy-eyed unbroken horse between them, roped from both sides. There was dust as well as heat.

Batista forgot about the Mexican woman and went over to lean on corral stringers to watch as the *vaqueros* inched their fighting, balky big colt towards a massive snubbing-post sunk four feet in the ground and standing in the centre of the corral.

Jose let a little slack lie in his rope. The horse lunged before Jose could take up the slack around the post, struck him in the shoulder with a foreleg, and when he fell the horse whirled. Gonzalo could do nothing. Batista yelled and scrambled into the corral, darted where the tag-end of Jose's riata was lying and grabbed it.

The horse did not turn on him until he had made an extra loop around the snubbing-post before hauling up on the slack. Gonzalo yelled and threw himself backwards to keep the horse from getting as far from the post as Batista, but he only had one wrap. When a thousand pounds of fighting heft came to the end of Gonzalo Gutierrez's riata, smoke rose from the tight wrap around the post.

The horse struck at Batista, missed, and spun to kick. Batista was moving backwards. The kick missed. Batista yelled for Gutierrez to yank his slack, which was done, then Batista slapped at the horse with his riata to make him move ahead far enough so that Batista could also gather slack.

The fighting horse did not jump ahead as most horses would have done when the lariat stung his rump, he whirled and this time when he hurled his full weight at the *mayordomo* he demonstrated the flaw of rawhide riatas. It broke, the horse nearly stumbled, Batista was twisting to flee when the big colt recovered, rushed ahead and stopped to sit back and strike.

He caught the *mayordomo* in the middle of the back. He went down under the impact, dust spurted, and Gonzalo Gutierrez dropped his tag-end, got between the horse and the unconscious older man, kicked dust at him, threw his hat into the animal's face, and when it retreated Gonzalo lifted Batista Moraga like a child, carried him to the gate, through it, hoisted him to his shoulder so that he could re-chain the gate, then walked away from the corral.

CHAPTER THIRTEEN

THE FAT WOMAN

The night was warm and alive with flickering stars when a woman almost as broad as she was tall came to the bedside to hold a candle low. Otherwise there were four other candles in the small adobe room where Batista Moraga lay on his handmade bed which was bolted to the wall.

The woman made a faint clucking sound. 'If your eyelids flicker from light you are alive. *Mayordomo,* stick out your tongue if you are hungry.'

The tongue immediately appeared. The woman's teeth shone in the gloom. 'How long have you been awake?'

'Since sundown,' admitted Moraga, and opened both eyes to her face. 'Carmelita, I would like some water.'

'Yes. With tequila in it?'

'Yes. Am I injured?'

'Is your back sore?'

'Yes. Sore as a boil.'

'That is where the horse struck you. You should do nothing for several days.'

'How is Jose?'

'Fine. He is fine. He and Gonzalo were here after you got hurt. They were worried, *mayordomo.*'

'Wasn't Jose struck the same way?'

'Yes, but it can be much worse with old men.'

'Carmelita, first the water, then something to eat.' While he had been speaking Batista had been edging his right hand close. When it was close enough he said, 'Old men?' and pinched hard with two fingers. The fat woman squealed, sprang away and turned with surprising agility for someone her size.

She brought his water laced with liquor, refused to meet his gaze and retreated hurriedly, indignantly, and in total silence.

He had the glass half emptied when voices

beyond his sight made murmurings of undistinguishable sounds. He hurriedly drained the glass and was putting it aside when Doña Elena entered the little room with its four candles.

She was no longer attired for horsebacking, so clearly she had returned from Hidalgo earlier. She approached the bed, looked down, met his smile and pulled up a chair Batista had made. It had four uneven legs and a fine rawhide seat.

He watched her with a dawning anxiety. She was not ready to speak until she was seated and composed and they had eye contact again. 'The woman is at the main-house with Rosalind to look after her.'

Batista squinted in the weak light to read her expression. 'And, *Señora*...?'

'Before I got there the *curandera* had washed her wounds and packed them with green fungus and bandaged them beneath a poultice of boiled mud.'

Batista knew that direct, fatalistic stare he was getting from having seen it before when something inevitable and probably very bad was going to occur. He sighed, let his mouth droop and drifted his dark gaze to the ceiling because this was expected of him, he knew it was, and as he had done before, he assumed the look of someone who was resigning himself to the worst.

Doña Elena changed the topic. 'They told

me how you were injured. Now maybe you can tell me why it is that the man in charge who had plenty of other men around feels that he has to do dangerous things himself?'

He looked back at her speaking Spanish. 'It was not dangerous.'

She answered in the same language. 'Then what are you doing on your back in that bed?'

He was irritated. 'Resting.'

She arose with a flourish and pushed the chair away. 'Then stop resting and stand up.'

Their eyes locked. Batista's irritation became slow and angry resolve. Holding his face absolutely expressionless he moved around until both feet were down, then stood up. The pain was bad. In poor light she could not see beads of sweat on his face.

She watched for a moment, then softly smiled at him. 'Pifas is outside. They are preparing your supper. I must go back and see our guest. By the way, her name is—'

'I know what her name is, *Señora*. For a favour, tell her Batista Moraga prays for her.'

Doña Elena departed, the fat woman appeared with a huge glazed adobe platter of food and right behind her was Pifas Garcia. He looked wan even by candlelight, wan and strained, tired and troubled. He ignored the woman, the food, even Batista until he had dropped down upon the chair and dumped his hat on the ground. Then instead of speaking he groaned.

Batista eased gingerly back down upon the bed, put the food aside and grunted at the fat woman as he held aloft his empty glass. She took it at arms' distance and fled.

Batista said, 'What is it, companion?'

'She is feverish. Part of the time on the wagon ride out here she did not know me. The *gringo* doctor said that if gangrene doesn't set in he will be astonished. Batista...?'

'Wait. Never mind the *gringo* doctor. Did you ever hear of a *gringo* doctor who could work miracles? Well, neither have I. So—here, drink this. It is tequila and water—so go to your house, get down and pray very hard. I will do the same.' Batista retrieved the empty glass and handed it back to the expressionless fat woman 'Another one, for favour, Carmelita. Strong, please, this time. Epifanio?'

The burly younger man arose with an effort, retrieved his hat and looked at the doorway as he softly said, 'I couldn't live with it if she died, Batista.'

Moraga considered one of the candles in its wall-niche. 'Go and pray. Come to see me in the morning. Good night.'

After Garcia left the fat woman appeared again, this time smiling as she put forth the refilled glass. Its alcoholic content, which was the same colour as water, made the glass appear to be full of pure water.

When Batista threw back his head and swallowed twice before choking, the fat woman shrilled with laughter and ran out of the room.

Later, when the yard was nearly as quiet as it ever was, Gonzalo Gutierrez came to visit briefly before bedding down. He told Batista that *Señor* Burket and his riders would bring the horses in the morning.

He also mentioned the Mexican woman, saying the general opinion was that she would die. Maybe not for a day or two, but soon.

Batista picked up his water glass, offered it to Gonzalo who declined, then drank it half empty before putting the glass aside again. He had to breathe through his mouth in deep sweeps for a moment. Poor visibility hid from the sight of Gonzalo that his eyes were watering.

Gonzalo had something else to say. 'The man who drove the wagon back with *la señora* said people in Mex town say General Martinez was very angry because there was soft lead jammed into the magazines of the Gatling gun.'

Batista accepted that. It did not surprise him.

Gonzalo continued. 'They said he organised his army after chasing the *federales* away and started marching towards the border.'

Moraga eyed the half-empty glass, decided against another drink and turned his attention back to Gutierrez. 'He looked like a foolish man, Gonzalo.'

'Do you want me to tell you how foolish, *jefe*?'

'He crossed the border with his raggedy-pantsed army?'

'That's not how he proved he was a fool, Batista. He started across without having scouts out. He was riding up ahead with his staff. Behind him were the cannoneers who had charge of pulling along his Gatling gun. He rode about a mile straight into an ambush by an American patrol that had been reinforced because they had heard the firing south of the border.'

Batista grinned. 'And...?'

'The *norteamericanos* also had a Gatling gun. When they rode away they had two Gatling guns, but theirs would fire and the other one still had lead in its magazines. They also had General Martinez and his staff. The rest of his army they told to get back south of the line and they did, in a big hurry.'

Gonzalo smiled, put his hat on and waited, but the *mayordomo* simply said, 'Good night,' and hoisted his legs atop the bed, composed himself, and, wearing a faint smile, closed his eyes.

Gutierrez went through to the balmy night with its fading scent of piñon smoke, saw the scarlet glow of a cigarette and went towards it.

It was the fat woman named Carmelita. She showed a beautiful smile when Gonzalo approached. 'Rosalind says the Mexican woman is very handsome.

Gutierrez leaned in night gloom. Rosalind was *la señora*'s housekeeper. 'What else does she say?' he asked.

Carmelita inhaled, exhaled, dropped her brown-paper smoke and ground it underfoot before replying. 'She said the woman's name is Maria Teresa Holquin y Bohorquez.'

Gonzalo saw the sly, teasing expression and responded to it. 'That is a matter of profound importance, sweetheart, but it is much too long for a gravestone.'

Carmelita switched to English, no longer smiling. 'She's not going to die. Where did you get such a crazy idea?'

'From the man who drove the wagon out here with the woman in it. He said the doctor in Hidalgo said she don't have one chance in five hunnert.'

Carmelita hitched her bulk around looking for something to sit on. There was nothing. Out front of the *mayordomo*'s residence there was the customary wooden bench bolted to the wall. Where Carmelita and Gonzalo were standing was on the south side of the *jacal*.

She led the way around the front. Gonzalo followed, eyed her rolling stride and rolled up his eyes, but when they were seated around in front he said, 'How can she live? When I saw her last she looked terrible.'

'So would you with bullet wounds. In fact you almost look terrible without them. She will live. She has to live. Everyone wants her to. *La señora* has candles lighted. Pifas has them too. I will have and so will others in a little while.' She turned on him. 'You always want the worst.'

Gutierrez blinked in surprise. 'I don't want the worst. What are you talking about?'

Carmelita rocked up to her feet and glared downwards. 'Then go home and pray. Go on, you rider of other people's horses!'

Gonzalo walked away through thick dust impressed by the indignation he had aroused in the fat woman, not quite able to understand it and, by the time he reached his own residence, not willing to make any further attempt to understand it.

Of one thing he was certain: The Mexican woman would die.

His final glance around held him motionless in the doorway for a moment. From the small window in the *jacal* of Pifas Garcia there was soft, warm-shaded glowing light. It was not being made by one votary candle but by several.

Gonzalo shrugged, entered his house,

tossed aside his hat and rummaged in a cupboard. There were extra candles there. He lighted four of them and knelt to pray.

The same weak, warm glow showed from other windows and doorways around the sprawling yard. One *jacal* showed no light at all and it belonged to the man who had said he would offer a prayer too, but between tequila, pain, exhaustion and age, the *mayordomo* had forgotten to pray. He was sleeping like the dead, without a sound or movement.

CHAPTER FOURTEEN

HORSES

Driving loose horses is neither an easy nor a routine affair, especially if they have eaten well and rested. It requires more men to herd fifty horses than it does to drive twice that many cattle. And in dry country there is dust. A *vaquero* doing chores saw the dust and routed out his companions. Batista, whose back was mildly painful, had wet eyes and a rattling headache when he shuffled to the barn area and gave orders: The corral gates were to be opened, the working horses confined there were to be put in other places, except for the animals the men were to ride.

147

They had enough time; the dust was clearly visible by morning sunlight but it was not very close. Pifas helped put the *vaqueros* out where they could turn the oncoming loose-stock.

Doña Elena, whose attention had been caught by the heavy drumroll of many hooves, came to her patio gate to watch as John Burket's riders appeared eerily through the dust, only one of them bringing up the rear, the others fanned out on both sides of the band.

Shouts rang distantly as Burket's horsemen alerted the yard ahead of their arrival, which was an unnecessary thing to do but it was customary.

Southeastward, well to the rear and far to one side of the approaching drive of horses, there was a top-buggy making a far less impressive banner of dust. Evidently the driver of the buggy chose to delay his arrival in the yard until the horses had been corralled. No one heeded the rig.

Jose Duarte, who was sitting astride to the west with a young rider, said, 'To arrive here this early they must have left the Burket ranch before daylight.'

The younger horseman nodded. 'Yes. Do you see the buggy?'

Jose had watched it briefly. 'I can guess,' he said. 'It will be the doctor from Hidalgo. They are like buzzards; they can smell it

148

when someone with money takes in an injured person.'

The horses, down to a rough trot now, hemmed on both sides by riders, made a large circling curve to go out and around the yard and come southwards in the direction of the corrals. The job was concluded perfectly. When the last horse was through the gate the men piled off to lean on corral stringers and relax. For Burket's men it had been a long drive.

Batista and the others of Alvarado Ranch mingled with the visitors. Someone mentioned coffee and the entire mob of horsemen went trooping away from the corrals.

John Burket crossed through settling dust in the direction of the *hacienda*. Doña Elena met him at the patio gate with a smile. Burket crossed to the old wooden bench, sank down pulling off his riding-gloves, and as Doña Elena sat down near by he said, 'They're not bad stock. Only a few have those spidery Mex brands, so we figure they were stolen up here not too long ago. There are a couple with army neck-brands.' He met her gaze with a twinkle. 'You can send 'em back to the soldiers or you can wait until they come for them, if they ever do.'

She said, 'Have you had breakfast?'

He nodded. 'Hours ago. But coffee would set well.' He paused to glance in the direction of the gate. 'We saw a buggy on the way in. I think it just crossed your yard.'

She arose and went to the gate. He studied her from the middle distance. She was statuesque. He knew she was a beautiful woman. He had seen her a number of other times, knew her to smile at and nod to when they met, but otherwise he'd relied on local information to form his opinion of her, and right now he wondered if what he had heard was not correct. She was stunning. He also got the impression that she was imperious. Perhaps it was her stance, or possibly it was her very direct, almost brusque way of speaking.

When she returned from the gate she had Paul Hudson with her. Doctor Hudson and John Burket were friends of long standing. John arose grinning and pumped the medical practitioner's hand. Hudson said, 'I thought that was your outfit driving those horses. How are you, John?'

'Holding together, Paul.'

Doña Elena took the medical man into the house and when she returned and he was still sitting in the shade, he said, 'I thought you were fetching the coffee.'

She blinked, reddened, turned without a word and went back inside. Burket relaxed, dropped his hat, shoved out his legs and through the half-droop of eyelids, listened to the sounds around him.

Elena returned with two cups of black java. One she handed to Burket, the other she kept in her right hand as she sat down while saying, 'Did you know I brought the Mexican woman out here from town?'

He sipped, blew on the coffee and nodded. 'Yes'm. I guess everyone in town knows that. How is she?'

'Would you care to see her?'

He looked up, startled. 'Isn't she dying?'

'I don't know. But she is lucid.' For a moment the handsome woman gazed at her coffee, then a faint smile appeared down around her mouth. 'Doctor Hudson is fit to be tied.'

'Why?'

She told him of the *curandera*. He listened, sipped coffee and said nothing. He had not been in the Hidalgo country very long, about eight years, but he had been born and raised in another part of the Southwest.

Elena raised her eyes to his bronzed, thoughtful profile. 'He had to cleanse her injuries. They had been treated with mould and boiled mud. The smell was terrible.'

John Burket looked up slowly. 'Yeah. It usually is.'

'You've seen this treatment before?'

He put down the cup, rolled up a sleeve and exposed a long white scar on his left forearm. 'I got that years ago at a marking-ground. An old Mex cow with horns from here to there caught me. It don't look bad now but it was a real mess when I got it.'

Elena leaned. 'Are you going to tell me a *curandera* took care of it?'

He was lowering his sleeve as he answered. 'Yes'm. She liked to send me straight through the roof. To clean it she used pulque. Then she packed in that mould. Two days later it smelt so bad I had flies followin' me even on horseback.'

He paused to smile at her. 'After the stuff was cleaned out and she washed it again with pulque, I'm here to tell you, Missus Alvarado, in four days it was practically all healed.'

Elena looked steadily at him for a long moment before speaking. 'Pure luck, Mister Burket.'

He did not look up from buttoning his cuff. He simply said, 'Tell me something: Do you know what a coincidence is?'

'Certainly. It's something that happens every now and then. Rarely and unpredictably.'

He laconically agreed. 'Yes'm. Something that happens rarely. Well now, I've seen injuries worse than I got on this arm cured an' healed by *curanderas* since I was big enough to have my eyes open.' Finally, he looked at her. 'One coincidence after another.' He jerked his head in the direction

152

of the house. 'The girl in there an' her stinkin' bandage; I'd say that's a coincidence. They all smell real bad while the medicine is pullin' out the infection. Want to hear my guess about another coincidence, ma'am?' John Burket leaned to retrieve his coffee cup. 'If she's still here four days from now she'll be mighty hard to keep down on her back in a bed.'

He drank the cup empty, put it between them on the bench and smiled at her as he arose. 'Thanks for your hospitality. Now I'd better round up my crew and—'

She interrupted him as she also arose from the bench. 'You can't leave. Wait until your men and animals are rested. My *vaquero*s will look after them. Is there a need for you to ride back during the hottest part of the day?'

There really wasn't, but John Burket was one of those people who, when they finished one job, wanted to get started on the next one. Except that at this time of year there was nothing pressing. He held his hat, gazing at her. He knew what he would have liked to say to her. Instead he mentioned Pifas Garcia's concern for the Mexican woman.

Elena had heard about this from several people. She accepted it. In fact, after considering it over a period of time, she liked the idea of the family-less woman and the restless *vaquero* being together. What had kept her tight wound was the possibility of

153

Maria Teresa dying. It had been a shattering thought. Now, gazing at the man before her, recalling his words about *curanderas*, she felt both relieved and grateful.

She said, 'Come with me. I think she will be glad to see you. Several times she talked about you.'

He nodded slowly. 'But mostly about Pifas Garcia.'

Elena Alvarado was turning towards the massive door when she laughed. 'Yes. Mostly about Pifas Garcia.'

The house was blessedly cool. Its three-foot-thick adobe walls kept heat out as well as sound. John Burket was conscious of the noise his spurs made as he followed Doña Elena through a huge parlour, sparsely furnished as was the custom, and down a long, gloomy hallway to an open door on the south side where sunlight came through the only window, recessed, grilled, and narrow.

Someone, probably Doña Elena's housekeeper, had burned piñon incense to overcome the smell of the pulpy mass of the *curandera*'s poultice on the floor. Doctor Hudson was returning a blue bottle to his little satchel when they entered the room. John Burket knew that little blue bottle. He did not have to stand close to Paul Hudson to know that he, not his patient, had swallowed some of the 'medicine' from the bottle.

154

Maria Teresa's dark eyes were very bright, almost feverish bright. She smiled at Doña Elena and John Burket. She was scrubbed, her mass of black hair shone from washing. Her colour was pale, but she was not dark so John, who looked for signs of a flush, was reassured.

As Doña Elena went to the side of the bed to lean and place a cool palm upon the woman's forehead, Burket looked across at Paul Hudson. The doctor rolled up his eyes without speaking.

Maria Teresa's eyes glistened as she murmured in English to Doña Elena. Hudson jerked his head behind them and led Burket out to the shadowy, cool, long corridor. Out there he spoke quietly. 'I know. You've shown me that scar on your arm. You've lived among these people so long you're more Mex than *gringo*.'

John smiled. 'All right, *gringo*, tell me.'

'Damnedest thing. I could smell it before I removed the poultice. Even the boiled mud was black.'

John said, 'That's the poison that's been sucked out.'

Doctor Hudson squinted. 'Do you really believe that?'

Burket made a motion as though to unbutton his cuff and the medical man stopped him. 'If I have to hear that story one more time...'

John did not raise the sleeve. He said, 'Paul, why do you have to disbelieve so hard?'

'Because it's no better than witchcraft.'

'All right, it's witchcraft. Now tell me, how did her wounds look after you cleaned them?'

'Well, you can't say that luck don't play a big part in—'

'Better, eh?'

Doctor Hudson glanced briefly in the direction of the doorway, then back. 'Better, yes.'

John did not press it, but he smiled at his friend and gave a typically Mexican shrug of the shoulders. 'It is healing?'

'Yes, but damned if I know why.'

'No infection?'

'None I could find.'

'She will live?'

'Did anyone say she wouldn't?'

'Quite a few people said she wouldn't.'

Hudson looked annoyed. 'People who know a lot about such things, no doubt. Every livery barn and pool hall has experts. Not just on medicine, on politics, the weather—'

John Burket interrupted. 'Paul, stay down here another five years and you'll have to accept that *curandera* medicine likely has about the same percentage of successes and failures as your kind.'

Hudson cleared his throat, stood briefly in thought, then smiled. 'I'll stay with my kind.'

Burket did not disagree. 'Sure. So will I. In fact I'll stay with both kinds.'

He left Doctor Hudson in the hallway, went back through the big, soundless old house to the patio, and crossed in the direction of the corrals.

Batista saw him approaching and went to meet him with raised brows and a quizzical look. Burket told him what the *gringo* doctor had said and Batista went in haste over towards a particular *jacal*.

He did not reappear at the corrals for a half-hour, by which time Pifas Garcia had gone to the main-house. Burket was leaning in barnshade among lounging horsemen, and watched the *mayordomo* approach, guessed where he had been and what he had done, but said nothing, only smiled at Moraga and jutted his jaw in the direction of the corrals. 'Maybe not as good as the ones you lost, but not typical Mex horses either.'

Batista had already looked the animals over. 'We thank you for making a good cut and driving them over.'

Burket said, '*Por nada, compañion.*'

Carmelita the fat woman came to say the women were preparing a large meal which would be ready in half an hour. She then looked pointedly at Batista Moraga and said in English that much delay would allow the men time to wash; that some would need more time for this than others. Then she departed.

John Burket raised his eyebrows. 'She don't like you, *mayordomo*?'

'It's not that. Last night I pinched her for saying I was an old man.

Burket nodded. 'Where did you pinch her?'

Batista turned back in the direction of the corral as he spoke. 'Some of those horses have army brands. Did you notice that?'

Burket gazed at the horses as though unaware that the *mayordomo* had changed the subject. He squinted. 'Yeah, we saw them. I told your lady you could take them back to the soldiers or wait until the soldiers came after them, if they ever did.'

Batista nodded, still looking in the direction of the horses. 'Are you married?'

Burket's eyes widened in surprise. 'Me? No. Why did you ask?'

The *mayordomo* finally turned his head in Burket's direction and smiled. 'Neither is Pifas Garcia. Not yet anyway.' He left John Burket in the shade and walked over to lean in sunlight upon the corral where several of the *vaqueros* were.

Burket went searching for a trough to wash in. Several of his riders followed this example. While they were drying off the fluting sound of someone pealing a brass bell

158

sounded across the yard. Without waiting all the *vaqueros* turned in the direction of the sound and as Batista Moraga led the way, he called to Burket and his riders that a meal was ready.

While the riders were occupied at three long trestle tables Doctor Hudson headed in the direction of Hidalgo in his top-buggy. The heat was building, had been increasing for several hours.

Doña Elena had asked the doctor to stay and eat. He had declined, saying the press of business required his return to town. His real reason for declining was that although he had lived a number of years in the Southwest, had even adopted many native customs, and might in time even arrive at a compromise between his profession and that of *curanderas*, it was going to take longer for him to live with southwestern food.

CHAPTER FIFTEEN

A SOFT TIME

It was characteristic of native South-westerners that meals for large numbers of people be turned into something like a fiesta. Without the dancing, music and drinking, but not without the peals of laughter, the loudness and comradeship.

John Burket understood this, as did most of his riders. They adapted as perfectly as men would who enjoyed this kind of thing. Particularly today; they had reason to celebrate.

The food was beef cooked over a deep pit atop a thick steel netting. There was no fire, just the intense heat of piñon burls, and long after the meal was finished, people sat in comfortable relaxation and sipped watered red wine as they smoked and talked.

Batista's headache left, he brought roars of laughter as he pretended to pursue the fat woman named Carmelita, holding his arms extended, his hands curled into the shape of pincers.

Carmelita did not laugh because she was not sure he did not intend to pinch her in front of everyone. She fled in red-faced disarray and only halted when she was in the doorway of a nearby building where she turned, panting, trying to shriek imprecations, but she could not do it without pauses to pull down great gulps of air.

The day was wearing along, John Burket's ranch was east of Hidalgo, which was a long ride. Before leaving the others he told one of his riders it might be a good idea if they headed home, and crossed to the hacienda to thank Doña Elena for her hospitality.

Her housekeeper left him standing in the

cool parlour while she went to Maria Teresa's room where her mistress was visiting the Mexican woman.

When Doña Elena appeared in the hall's arched entrance to the parlour John Burket stopped, idly turning the hat he was holding in both hands.

Elena Alvarado was attired in a split riding-skirt of silk-soft split-hide buckskin, a white blouse, and high, dark boots. She looked ready to ride. She smiled faintly and offered John Burket a chair. He remained standing as he thanked her for all she had done, and when she gave the Spanish equivalent of a deprecatory remark, '*Por nada*', he smiled. If she had also shrugged it would have been typical. But she did not shrug, she crossed the big room and halted about ten feet in front of him where he picked up the faint scent of clean hair rinsed in some kind of flower-water.

He asked about the Mexican woman. Her answer was forthright, which was what he had come to expect from her. She did not appear to be indecisive about anything. 'She is resting well.'

Then she grinned and sat down looking up at him. 'I'm afraid I'll never be able again to scoff at *curanderas*, Mister Burket.'

He nodded slightly, eyes smiling back. 'That's the first step in becoming a native.'

She held his gaze. 'What is the next step?'

161

His eyes slid away from her face. The next step, of course, was to have a husband and many children. He skirted a direct answer by saying, 'Oh, I guess it's to find reasons for accepting things, rather than doubting them.'

This time she laughed. He was uncomfortable. She thought she knew why. 'I do accept things. After all I've been here long enough for that.' She leaned, arms on her upper legs, eyeing him thoughtfully. 'I don't think you've ever been married,' she told him, and startled him exactly as Batista Moraga had down at the corrals.

With faint colour rising he replied. 'You're right, I never have.'

'It's lonely, isn't it, Mister Burket?'

He eyed her steadily for a long moment and did not give a direct reply. 'My name is John. I guess it'd be lonely if a person had time for loneliness, Missus Alvarado.'

Her steady dark gaze never wavered. 'Your name is John, mine is Elena.' She arose and moved towards the massive oak mantel above a huge stone fireplace, turned with her back to it and put her steady gaze upon him. She could be disconcertingly direct, but at this moment she was disconcerting in another way. She would have been stunning even in harsh sunlight, but standing against the dark old stonework of the huge fireplace in her riding-skirt, boots, white blouse, and

162

with her mass of dark hair held in back by a small ribbon, she had him speechless.

'I owe you for the horses, and for everything else you have done, John. I'll tell you something I've heard at least a hundred times since I've been here, and never believed until those border-jumpers stole our animals. This is a man's country.'

He neither nodded nor spoke, just stood gazing at her.

Elena Alvarado breathed a soundless sigh. He was a handsome man, as resolute as stone and just about as thick. She remained by the fireplace when she said, 'But no one lives by bread alone, do they?'

His gaze wavered as he wanted to believe what might be the meaning behind her words, but was fearful of saying something which would be inappropriate if his interpretation was incorrect. John Burket lacked subtlety. 'It'll be a long ride back,' he told her. 'My men will be saddling up.'

She remained in place looking steadily at him. Then she made a little fluttery gesture of defeat with both hands and spoke briskly, the softness gone. 'I want to pay my share of the cost of the expedition down into Mexico.'

He thought about that. 'Well, maybe one of these days you could have a fiesta for everyone who went down there. That's the custom.'

She nodded. 'We'll do that, but there is still the out-of-pocket expense.'

He grinned broadly. '*Por nada*,' he said, and they both laughed.

She crossed the room towards him. 'You could send your men back and stay here for supper with me.'

This time he met her direct dark gaze with no inhibitions between them. 'I could.'

'Will you?'

'If you want me to.'

'Then do it. After they are gone you and I could take the horses out a few miles on the range and leave them with my other loose-stock.'

He nodded and abruptly left the house heading for the barn. She watched from the patio with a lowering sun made coppery by dust shadowing the front of the big house and the patio.

The housekeeper came to the door. Doña Elena smiled at her. '*Señor* Burket will be here for supper.'

The woman nodded and went to her kitchen. She stopped once to look over her shoulder, and broadly smiled.

Batista Moraga and Epifanio Garcia came to the barn's front opening with John Burket. They stood silently and watched him cross back in the direction of the main-house. Batista brushed Garcia's arm as he said, 'It's about time.'

Pifas nodded. 'Past time, friend. By the way, I want to thank you for praying for Maria Teresa last night. There were many prayers. You see, exactly as my grandmother told me, good prayers are answered. So are the other kind, but usually the answer is—no.'

Batista shot his companion a quick look. He had completely forgotten to pray last night. While Garcia was watching the *gringo* across the yard near the patio gate where Doña Elena was waiting, wearing a smile, Batista Moraga rolled his eyes upwards, and shrugged. No one was perfect; everyone forgets things. *He* would understand. The most difficult thing on earth, as *He* well knew, was to be a *gente de razón*, an animal who reasons.

Photoset, printed and bound in Great Britain by REDWOOD BOOKS, Trowbridge, Wiltshire